Stolen Magic

Dragon's Gift: The Huntress Book 3

Linsey Hall

DEDICATION

For Catherine Bowler, one of the smartest, kindest, most genuine people I know. The world is vastly better because you are in it.

ACKNOWLEDGMENTS

Thank you, Ben, for everything you've done to support me. Thank you to Carol Thomas for sharing your thoughts on the book and being amazing inspiration. My books are always better because of your help.

The Dragon's Gift series is a product of my two lives: one as an archaeologist and one as a novelist. I'd like to thank my friends, Wayne Lusardi, the State Maritime Archaeologist for Michigan, and Douglas Inglis and Veronica Morris, both archaeologists for Interactive Heritage, for their ideas about how to have a treasure hunter heroine that doesn't conflict too much with archaeology's ethics. The Author's Note contains a bit more about this if you are interested

Thank you to Jena O'Connor and Lindsey Loucks for various forms of editing. The book is immensely better because of you! And thank you to Kathy Neibarger, who caught several embarrassing errors in the final manuscript.

GLOSSARY

Alpha Council - There are two governments that enforce law for supernaturals—the Alpha Council and the Order of the Magica. The Alpha Council governs all shifters. They work cooperatively with Alpha Council when necessary - for example, when capturing FireSouls.

ArchMage - The greatest mage of that particular skill. For example, the ArchMage of Fire Mages. There can also be an ArchWitch or ArchSorcerer.

Blood Sorceress - A type of Magica who can create magic using blood.

Conjurer - A Magica who uses magic to create something from nothing. They cannot create magic, but if there is magic around them, they can put that magic into their conjuration.

Dark Magic - The kind that is meant to harm. It's not necessarily bad, but it often is.

Deirfiúr - Sisters in Irish.

Demons - Often employed to do evil. They live in various hells but can be released upon the earth if you know how to get to them and then get them out. If they are killed on earth, they are sent back to their hell.

Dragon Sense - A FireSoul's ability to find treasure. It is an internal sense pulls them toward what they seek. It is easiest to find gold, but they can find anything or anyone that is valued by someone.

Elemental Mage – A rare type of mage who can manipulate all of the elements.

Enchanted Artifacts – Artifacts can be imbued with magic that lasts after the death of the person who put the magic into the artifact (unlike a spell that has not been put into an artifact—these spells disappear after the Magica's death). But magic is not stable. After a period of time—hundreds or thousands of years depending on the circumstance—the magic will degrade. Eventually, it can go bad and cause many problems.

Fire Mage – A mage who can control fire.

FireSoul - A very rare type of Magica who shares a piece of the dragon's soul. They can locate treasure and steal the gifts (powers) of other supernaturals. With practice, they can manipulate the gifts they steal, becoming the strongest of that gift. They are despised and feared. If they are caught, they are thrown in the Prison of Magical Deviants.

The Great Peace - The most powerful piece of magic ever created. It hides magic from the eyes of humans.

Half-blood - A supernatural who is half one species and half another. Example: shifter and Magica.

Heart of Glencarrough - The child who tends the Heartstone.

Hearth Witch – A Magica who is versed in magic relating to hearth and home. They are often good and potions and protective spells and are also very perceptive when on their own turf.

Heartstone - A charm that protects Glencarrough, the Alpha Council stronghold, from dark magic. It was created through the sacrifice of many shifters and must be tended by the Heart of Glencarrough, a child.

Magica - Any supernatural who has the power to create magic—witches, sorcerers, mages. All are governed by the Order of the Magica.

Mirror Mage - A Magica who can temporarily borrow the powers of other supernaturals. They can mimic the powers as long as they are near the other supernatural. Or they can hold onto the power, but once they are away from the other supernatural, they can only use it once.

The Origin - The descendent of the original alpha shifter. They are the most powerful shifter and can turn into any species.

Order of Holy Knowledge - A group of monks who collect and protect knowledge and who live on an island in Ireland. They are supernaturals, but they do not use their powers.

Order of the Magica - There are two governments that enforce law for supernaturals—the Alpha Council and the Order of the Magica. The Order of the Magica govern all Magica. They work cooperatively with Alpha Council when necessary - for example, when capturing FireSouls.

Phantom - A type of supernatural that is similar to a ghost. They are incorporeal. They feed off the misery and pain of others, forcing them to relive their greatest nightmares and fears. They do not have a fully functioning mind like a human or supernatural. Rather, they are a shadow of their former selves. Half bloods are extraordinarily rare.

Scroll of Truth - A compendium of knowledge about the strongest supernaturals. It is a prophetic scroll that includes information about future powerful beings.

Seeker - A type of supernatural who can find things. FireSouls often pass off their dragon sense as Seeker power.

Shifter - A supernatural who can turn into an animal. All are governed by the Alpha Council.

Transporter - A type of supernatural who can travel anywhere. Their power is limited and must regenerate after each use.

CHAPTER ONE

"Trouble at two o'clock." I tipped my chin toward the big glass window.

Nix glanced up from behind the counter and peered at the two figures crossing the street toward our shop, Ancient Magic. Rain fell on their huge forms as they stalked toward us. Her green eyes assessed them sharply.

My *deirfiúr*—sister by choice—was a pro at spotting danger. She normally worked the counter at Ancient Magic, a job that was just as much protecting the wares as it was selling them. She was basically the deadliest shopgirl you'd ever meet.

"Ah, hell. They're trouble." She pulled her dark hair back into a ponytail.

"Yeah. Gotta be demons." They were almost seven feet tall and built like moose. Unless a basketball team had had babies with a football team and their charming family was visiting town, these guys were demons.

A month ago, I'd have reached for the obsidian daggers I kept strapped to my thighs. I'd repressed my magic for so long that weapons had become second nature. But ever since I'd started practicing my magic, I'd gained confidence.

And I liked using my magic now. A lot.

The hulking demons stepped onto the curb. Through the glass, I could make out the sawed-off horns peeking through their hair and their strange silver eyes. Weird eyes. Their arms bulged out of sleeveless shirts that were totally stupid for a rainy Oregon afternoon. Besides the massive size and the horns, they looked almost human.

My eyes skated around the shop, landing on the delicate items displayed on the shelves. Each housed a spell, and most of them were worth a lot of money.

Whichever one these demons were coming for, they weren't going to get it.

"Can't we make it a month without a robbery?" Nix said.

"Where's the fun in that?" My brows rose as the demons turned away from our door and walked down the sidewalk. Like they hadn't even seen us.

"What the hell?" Nix got up from her stool and walked around the counter, peering out the window. "They're not coming in here?"

"Then it's not our problem."

"But it's not good either," Nix said.

I sighed. "Yeah. Fair point."

I didn't want them to bust up our shop in some dumb attempt at a robbery, but demons shouldn't be wandering around earth, not even in all magic cities like Magic's Bend, which was concealed from humans by a massive spell. Most demon species were too violent and reckless to follow the rules that kept supernaturals a secret from humans, so they were banned from earth.

"Too bad Del's not here," Nix said. "She'd take care of them."

"Yeah."

Del, my other *deirfiúr*, was a demon hunter paid by the Order of the Magica, the government that ruled magic users like myself. I could kick some demon ass, but I preferred not to unless I was being paid. Del enjoyed it, though. She'd take care of these guys as a way to pass the time.

"Hey, they're going into P&P!"

"What?" I sprang to my feet. Demons had no right being in Potions & Pastilles, my friends' coffee shop. "Now it's our problem."

"No kidding."

We hurried out of Ancient Magic. I started down the street, leaving Nix to reignite the enchantments that protected our shop. Couldn't have our stock walking away while we hunted demons, after all.

I slowed as I reached the huge front window outside Potions & Pastilles, then hovered just out of view and peered through the glass. The large coffee shop was empty of customers, the wooden tables and comfy chairs abandoned. Connor and Claire, my two friends who ran the shop, were behind the counter, tidying up before the evening rush. The demons approached them, stopping in front of the counter.

Did I need to bust in there and not bother to take names? But a bit of recon was worth a lot of fighting.

I called upon my magic, accessing the Shifter powers I'd recently stolen, and used them to enhance my hearing. I let the magic roll over me, filling me with warmth and igniting my power. Joy and pleasure flowed with it, something that had only recently started accompanying my magic. I assumed it was because I was more practiced and less afraid, but I didn't know.

The birds chirping in the trees became louder, the sound of Nix's approaching footsteps more prominent.

But it was the bigger demon's words that made my stomach drop.

"We've heard there are FireSouls in the area." His voice sounded like he spoke through a throat full of gravel. "We can find no trace of them, except for here, in your shop."

I reached out and grabbed Nix's arm to keep her from charging in front of the window. She whipped around and glared at me. Nix was more generally cautious than Del or me, but when it came to protecting those she loved, she was a freaking badger.

I shook my head, tapped my ear to indicate I was eavesdropping, and dragged her behind the wall so we weren't right in front of the window. The demons wouldn't hurt Connor or Claire, not as long as they wanted information, and I wanted to know who'd sent them to find me and my *deirfiúr*.

Inside the coffee shop, Claire shook her head, her dark hair swinging. "FireSouls?" Her eyes widened. "Around here? In *our* shop?"

If I hadn't been frozen in place from fear, I'd have grinned. Claire was a good actress. My *deirfiúr* and I had revealed our secret to Connor and Claire a few days ago—that we were FireSouls, the most hated of all supernatural species.

Did that have anything to do with demons now showing up, looking for us?

No way my friends turned us in.

"Aye, can't you hear right?" the demon barked. "Around here. Deadly pieces of work. So if you don't want your power stolen by one of those monsters, you'd better share what you know. They'll kill you in a heartbeat to get your magic."

Not true. But I'd kill that demon in a heartbeat. And where did he get off calling me a monster?

FireSouls were despised—we could steal other supernatural's powers by killing them—but we weren't monsters. My *deirfiúr* weren't like that.

But me? Now that I'd started accessing my FireSoul power, I was afraid he might be right. When I'd stolen the Shifter's power recently, I hadn't been able to control myself. Maybe I was becoming as bad as they said, but I didn't like hearing it from a demon.

"No idea what you're talking about, mate," Connor said. "There's no way FireSouls have been in here."

The big demon surged toward the wooden counter, slamming his hands down. "You calling me a liar? Because a seer prophesied their presence and I tracked them here. Their magic reeks in this place."

Shit. A Tracker demon. I'd thought their weird eyes looked familiar but couldn't place them. They were like the bloodhounds of demons, easily able to sense other supernaturals' magic and follow it. Del, Nix, and I had always been scared of them, though we'd never met any face to face. If we had, our secret might be out by now, and we might be locked up in the Prison for Magical Miscreants.

The other demon drew a wicked-looking knife from the sheath strapped to his massive arm.

Nix tugged against my hold, her face twisted into an exasperated *What the hell are we waiting for!?*

She was right. It was one thing to listen for info. Another entirely to put my friends in danger.

"Go time," I whispered.

We raced forward, shoulder to shoulder. By the time we pushed through the glass door, the demon had Connor by the collar, dragging his slim form over the counter. Connor threw a mean right hook, but the demon didn't even flinch.

Stone demon as well as Tracker? Halfbloods weren't unheard of.

A flash of silver to his left caught my eye. Claire, a mercenary as well as a part-time coffee shop owner, had dragged a sword from beneath the counter. She leapt over the bar, her dark hair flying, and lunged for the other demon.

The scent of flowers bloomed as Nix called upon her magic and conjured a wicked-looking sword of her own. She raced to join Claire.

Though I wanted to fry the demon who shook Connor with the lightning that was becoming my signature power, I didn't want it to flow through to Connor and electrocute him too. So I pulled my daggers from the sheaths at my thighs, flinging Lefty and Righty in quick succession.

The black obsidian blades sank into the Tracker demon's back. He grunted and dropped Connor, but didn't fall.

Strong bastard.

But now that he wasn't touching Connor anymore...

I called upon my lightning, letting the power surge through my veins. It crackled and burned beneath my skin as I gathered it up. Joy filled me at my control, at the feeling of finally embracing my magic. Like my soul was coming together.

My breath caught in my throat as I focused my power, attempting not to go overboard. I wanted to wound, not kill, so I could question him.

I released the jet of lightning. Fine and direct, it streaked toward the demon. Thunder boomed as the lightning stuck. The demon's huge body shook, then collapsed to the floor. A chair crunched beneath him.

Direct hit! And almost no collateral damage. Jackpot. I grinned. I was really starting to like this magic thing.

At the same time, Nix and Claire sank their blades into both sides of the remaining demon. They yanked out their swords, and his huge body crashed to the floor. I raced toward the fallen demons as Connor struggled to his feet.

The demon I'd struck with lightning lay on his front, his body still smoking. I pulled my blades from his back and shoved him over. Sightless eyes stared at the ceiling.

"Definitely dead." Connor's voice was hoarse from being strangled.

Damn.

I'd tried not to kill him. Hadn't worked. But at least I hadn't killed Connor.

The second demon lay bleeding out onto the floor. I went to him, falling to my knees and straddling him, then thrust Righty against his throat. The black glass glinted in the light.

"Who sent you?" I demanded.

He choked, his features twisting at the pain of approaching death. The blood that welled from his chest felt warm against my legs. Gross.

His powers—those bloodhound Tracker senses and the massive strength that made him into a living stone—called to my own.

Covetousness surged, an aching hunger to steal his magic. He was so strong. *I* could be that strong. I didn't need any help finding things, but his strength would come in more than handy. Fire filled my body, a blazing heat that seared my soul. Hunger and need and desire rushed through me, a potent cocktail that stole my control.

I could take his strength, have it for my own. All I had to do was let my FireSoul take his power as he died. The need was so strong it ate me from within.

Shaking, I pressed my hands to his shoulders, my magic reaching out for his. White flame flickered across my skin, extending out to him. I tasted the iron of his magic as it flowed to me.

Joy seethed inside of me as I stole his power, sick and dark.

"Cass!" Nix's voice pinged in my head. "Cass! What are you doing?"

Nix's shout tugged at my conscience. I gasped, surfacing from the trance I'd fallen into. The white flame still flicked across my skin, reaching into the body beneath me.

I threw myself away from him, desperate to escape the force compelling me to steal his powers. I had no problem killing him—he'd threatened my friends—and little problem stealing his powers, but I wanted it to be a conscious decision. Not one that I was forced to make. Not one I enjoyed so much.

"Cass! Are you all right?" Nix asked. She fell to her knees beside me, concern in her gaze.

I shook my head, clearing my blurry vision. Shudders racked my body. The desperate hunger was fading now that I was away from him. I glanced at his body.

Dark eyes stared sightlessly at the ceiling. Dead.

No, I wasn't resisting. The hunger was fading because he was dead. I could no longer take his power, so the temptation was gone. It wasn't my own willpower or strength.

Damn. What was I turning into?

"Cass?" Nix's voice shook me from my thoughts.

"Yeah. Yeah, I'm fine."

"You don't look fine," Nix said.

I hadn't told Nix or Del about my new fear that my FireSoul compelled me to steal magic when I was in close proximity to a dying body. Or that I enjoyed it so much.

It made me a monster.

9

Like the one from my past who hunted me and my *deirfiúr*. It was one thing to take powers, but it was another thing entirely to enjoy it so much. To do it without control. Like an addict.

"No, I'm fine. I wanted to ask him questions, but he's dead." I climbed to my feet. "And I hate getting blood on my clothes."

"Yeah, all right," Nix said as she rose, but her gaze lingered on my. She was suspicious, but didn't say anything.

I wasn't off the hook. Nix was great at biding her time. She'd told me once that when I was stressed, I had the bad habit of shutting down. She usually just waited me out. Nix was the patient one.

I climbed to my feet as Nix and Claire turned to Connor. He was straightening his crumpled band t-shirt—*Amy MacDonald, live from Glasgow* today—and rubbing his throat. His face was still ruddy from air loss and his dark eyes bright, but he looked all right otherwise.

"That was one nasty piece of work," Connor said.

Connor was a Hearth Witch with a knack for potions, so hand-to-hand wasn't his specialty. He was a badass with potion bombs and a sword if he could get his hands on one, but this kind of fighting had never been his thing.

"We better hide these bodies until they disappear," I said. "Pull them behind the counter or something."

Connor frowned. "Yeah, that wouldn't be good for business. Would you like a side of dead demon with your triple boosted latte, madam?"

"Why, that sounds delightful," Nix said in a singsong voice as she grabbed a demon by the leg and dragged him behind the counter.

Please don't let the health inspector show up.

It wouldn't take long for the demons to disappear and return to the hell that they'd come from. You couldn't really kill a demon, just their earthly form. In a little while, they'd wake up in their hell.

But at least we didn't have to deal with their bodies, and whoever had hired them wouldn't be seeing them for a while.

"Thanks for covering for us," I said after I'd dragged the second demon's body behind the counter. "I have no idea how they found us. Whoever they were."

"They mentioned a seer. But didn't they come from your shop?" Claire asked. "They came from that direction at least."

"They couldn't see us," I said as Connor went behind the counter and started to make coffee. Back to business as usual. "We have concealment charms that hide us from the eyes of anyone seeking us with ill intent. It's how we've managed to stay hidden for so long."

My sisters and I had lived in Magic's Bend for five years, but we'd only been able to settle here once we bought the concealment charms. Without them, we'd have to stay on the run or risk the Monster from our past finding us.

"I'm sorry this brought trouble to your door," I said. "But we really appreciate you having our back."

"Yeah," Nix said. "You have no idea. We've never had friends like you before."

"That's what friends are for," Claire said. "Do you think those guys were sent by the Monster who hunts you?"

"Maybe." My skin crawled at the thought. My *deirfiúr* and I had no memory of the first fifteen years of our lives. Only that we were FireSouls and that we'd fled from someone terrible. I'd met him recently, so he knew we were still alive. "Probably."

My cell phone vibrated in my pocket. I dug my hand in and pulled it out, then glanced at the message displayed on the screen.

FOUND SOMETHING. MEET AT OFFICE.

I glanced up and met three pairs of expectant eyes.

"Dr. Garriso wants to talk to me," I said. "I'd better run."

Nix's eyes flared with interest. She knew I'd given our scholar friend the Chalice of Youth, an artifact linked to the Monster, and that I was waiting for answers. We wanted to know why the Monster hunted the chalice and hoped Dr. Garriso would be able to help us.

"Go, go," Nix said. "I'll hang out here and make sure these bodies disappear."

"I can handle that," Claire said. "I deal with enough demon bodies in my day job anyway. I've got the skill set."

"It's the least I can do," Nix said. "And this is my favorite place to eat. I don't want you getting shut down by the health inspector."

Claire laughed. The sound followed me as I headed out of the shop.

I stepped out into the late afternoon drizzle and turned toward my car, immediately bumping into a tall, hard form. I stiffened, muscles on high-alert, then stepped back and looked up.

Aidan.

I relaxed, then smiled. My heart jumped in my chest.

"Hey." He grinned down, his smile a slash of white in his handsome face.

His dark hair and the blue shirt he wore glittered with raindrops. It made him look even more like a model. The rugged kind, not the pretty kind. Though I appreciated both. I always felt vastly outclassed by him, but I'd learned to ignore it.

His magic surged against mine with the sound of waves crashing and the taste of chocolate. He smelled like the forest, and I had to stop myself from sucking in a deep breath.

A girl had to have some pride.

"Hey." I smiled up at him. "Long time no see."

My friend and maybe-boyfriend—honestly, I had no idea what to call him—had been gone on business for the last three days. I'd missed him.

"Sorry I was away longer than expected, but it's done," he said. His big hands gripped my shoulders, and heat shivered across my skin.

Aidan Merrick was the Origin, a descendent of the first Shifter and one of the most powerful supernaturals in the world. He was also a Magica with Elemental Mage powers and some healing ability. I'd met him about a month ago when he'd hired me to help him find a dangerous scroll. FireSouls can find just about anything of value, so I made my living finding valuable magic to sell at my shop. It was how Aidan had tracked me down.

After that job, he'd figured out I was a FireSoul—smart bastard—but instead of turning me in to the Order of the Magica, which would've resulted in a life sentence for me at the Prison for Magical Miscreants, he'd stuck by my side, helping me with a difficult job. Things had snowballed from there, though we'd never had any time for a real date or other romancey stuff.

Mostly, we'd been running for our lives or someone else's. At this point, I didn't even know what romancey stuff was. I'd have liked to figure it out, though.

"Yeah, well I can forgive you," I said. "You've sort of let your business lapse while you've been watching my back."

Aidan owned Origin Enterprises, a security business that made him immeasurably wealthy. At least by my standards.

"I like having your back." Aidan grinned.

The sight sucker punched me. Damn, he looked good.

When had I become so shallow?

"But you never returned my calls," he said. "Got anything to say for yourself?"

My stomach dropped. "Noticed that, did you?"

"Might have. Any reason why?"

Yeah, but none that I wanted to share. Ever since I'd stolen a Shifter's magic a week ago, I'd been so freaked out by my changing powers—and intense desire to steal other supernaturals' magic—that I'd done my usual. I'd shut down. I didn't know how to share with anyone besides my *deirfiúr*, and this felt too dark to share even with them. I hadn't felt like faking being okay on the phone. That felt like lying.

Though now that I looked at it from his perspective, disappearing hadn't been great either.

"I'm sorry. That was bad of me. I've got a good reason." I cringed. "Maybe not a good reason, but one that has nothing to do with you. It was all me. Being weird. I'm sorry."

"I like you weird. But I'd like you better if you talked to me."

"Fair enough. But later? I'm headed somewhere."

"Where to?" Aidan asked.

"Dr. Garriso wants to see me about the Chalice of Youth." My heart pounded at the idea of finally figuring out what it was. "So I've got to run. Meet you later tonight?"

"Why don't I come with?"

"Uhhh." I'd gotten used to having him at my side, but were we going to make it a regular thing? Would I like that?

There was only one way to find out. "Yeah, all right. Let's go. But I'm driving."

"Fine by me."

15

I turned to cross the street toward my old junker, but Aidan's hand caught my arm. I shivered. Gently, he pulled me back.

"Hang on." His voice sounded rough. "I haven't had a chance to do this yet."

My eyes darted up, meeting his dark gaze. Heat flared in its depths, igniting the same within me. He leaned down and pressed his lips to mine, stealing my breath. My head swam as his mouth moved against mine.

He was the best kisser—his lips soft and skilled and his taste divine. My heart threatened to break my ribs. Just as I clenched my fists in his shirt, he pulled away.

"Come on," he said. "Let's go find out about that chalice. You seemed excited."

What I was excited about was kissing him. Tension had raged between us for almost a month now, but between running for our lives and being called away by work, we hadn't had a chance to actually act on anything yet.

It was getting to be about damned time, if my heart rate was any indication.

"Yeah, let's go," I said. "Were getting rained on anyway."

"Oh, I could ignore the rain."

I grinned and punched him in the shoulder, then turned away.

We crossed the street quickly, heading toward the park on the other side. Ancient Magic and P & P were located on Factory Row, the recently revitalized old factory district of Magic's Bend. Rent was low and the company was weird, but that's what I liked about it.

We climbed into Cecelia, my old junker with chipped paint and a spotty engine. It sputtered and coughed as I cranked it, but when the engine finally turned over, I wanted to cheer.

"You know, you could afford a new car with your take from your last job," Aidan said.

I pulled onto the street. "Yeah, but I don't care about cars. Cecelia here will do me just fine."

The four million I'd made on my last job—a record haul even for me—was going toward increased concealment charms for myself and my *deirfiúr* and protection spells for our apartments and shop. Not to mention my trove.

FireSouls were said to share the soul of a dragon, though no one had seen a dragon in centuries. Considering the fact that my *deirfiúr* and I were as covetous as dragons eyeing a pile of gold, I believed it. We thought it was the dragon's covetousness that gave us our special sense for finding treasure. The rest of that four million would go towards padding my trove—a collection of leather jackets, boots, and weapons. It might be weird treasure, but it was mine.

It didn't take long to drive through Magic's Bend, a medium-sized city of supernaturals. We chatted about Aidan's trip as the tall buildings of the business district passed by in all their sterile glory, giving way to the quirky structures in the historic district where the good bars were located, and then by Darklane, where everybody knew the dark magic practitioners hung out.

"Here we are," I said as we pulled into the large parking lot at the Museum of Magical History. The rain had lightened up while we were driving, but I still sprinted towards the back door.

I tapped on Dr. Garriso's window as I passed, then headed toward the big gray door. Aidan joined me as we waited for Dr. Garriso to unlock it. We were here after hours, but you could always count on Dr. Garriso to be in his office. I wasn't entirely sure he didn't live there.

The door swung open, and the small white-haired figure of Dr. Garriso smiled at us. "Welcome, welcome. Come in."

We stepped out of the rain and followed him down the cold, boring hallway, which was nothing like the rest of the museum. Researchers always got the shaft.

Dr. Garriso was a small man, about seventy, and favored the tweed coats that made him look like an old Sherlock Holmes.

He pushed open the door to his office. As soon as I stepped over the threshold, I couldn't help but grin. It was like stepping back in time. Bookshelves lined every wall, stuffed to overflowing with ancient leather tomes and newer paperbacks. Old Tiffany lamps gleamed warmly from wooden tables, leather chairs invited, and the air smelled like tea.

How he'd turned the sterile researcher's office into this wonderland from a past century, I had no idea. But I liked it.

"Could I get you some tea?" Dr. Garriso asked. "I have a lovely new blend from India."

"Yes, please," I said.

I could never resist Dr. Garriso's tea. It wasn't my beloved Pabst Blue Ribbon—PBR for short, the beer of hipsters and hillbillies—but something about it suited his office so well that I could never say no. And now wasn't exactly the time for a cold one, anyway.

Aidan and I crossed the narrow space to the small seating area under the window. There were two plush leather chairs, but Aidan picked up a small wooden one in front of the bookshelves and brought it over. He fitted his huge form onto the seat, leaving the two nicer chairs for Dr. Garriso and me.

Not a bad dude.

"Thanks," I said as I sank into the leather chair.

Dr. Garriso puttered at the small table holding the electric kettle and his collection of tea supplies.

The kettle dinged, and he fussed some more, then carried the tea over on a tiny silver tray and set it on the table between the leather chairs. He turned and retrieved a leather box from a high shelf.

I reached for my tea as he opened the box, sipping and sighing gratefully at the added sweetness. Dr. Garriso knew I had the sweet tooth of a twelve-year-old. Five sugar cubes. It was a little ridiculous, but I didn't care.

"This is an interesting item," Dr. Garriso said as he removed the ornate golden chalice from the box.

Shiny.

The yellow metal glinted in the low light, and my fingers itched to touch it. Though I preferred a different type of treasure, the dragon in my soul couldn't help but covet anything that shiny.

"What is it?" I asked. "I know it can't just be a beauty charm."

19

Right before I'd met Aidan, I'd recovered the Chalice of Youth on a job, specifically for Mr. S, Magic Bend's favorite weatherman. Del, who consulted ancient records to determine which enchanted artifacts I would go after, had determined that the Chalice of Youth would do for Mr. S's needs.

But it'd turned out that the chalice was more than just a beauty charm. The Monster from my past had been hunting it as well. There was no way he'd have been hunting it if it weren't special.

"Well, you see," Dr. Garriso said. "It's a difficult object. It is definitely a beauty charm, but that spell was placed on the chalice to hide its true purpose. The chalice possesses a spell that allows whoever drinks from it—"

An enormous crash sounded from one of the floors above, followed by a shout. Magic swelled in the air, a bitter, burning aroma that was hard to identify. But it smelled like dark magic.

I surged to my feet, Aidan alongside me, his massive form graceful despite his size.

"What was that?" Dr. Garriso's white brows rose to touch his snowy hairline.

"Nothing good," I said.

"Not a robbery," Dr. Garriso said. "It can't be."

Pounding footsteps sounded on the floor above. A guard running? A thief?

"I don't know, but we'd better check it out," I said. I hated the idea of anyone coming in here and messing with the history contained within these walls. This stuff was irreplaceable. "We'll be right back, Dr. Garriso."

I raced from the room with Aidan. The sterile lights of the hallway burned my eyes after the dim pleasantness of Dr. Garriso's office. We sprinted side by side down the wide hallway, following the sound of crashing and yelling, and pushed through the doors at the end of the hall, spilling out into one of the main exhibit rooms.

The ceiling soared high above, the setting sun gleaming orange from behind the enormous glass windows. Marble statues dotted the space, but no people.

Another crash sounded.

"Left," I said.

We sprinted toward it, crossing through exhibits that held only artifacts. The sound of a fight beckoned, leading us to a moderately-sized room full of ancient vases and amphoras. Glass cases filled the space, gleaming dully in the light.

A purple portal glowed from the corner. Lavender light pulsed from it, illuminating the two figures who stood on either side, their arms outstretched, as if they were manipulating the magic that created the portal. They were Magica of some sort. Maybe demons, though some species looked human. Their power smelled like rot and decay, with a hint of the ocean behind it.

Dark magic covered their own signature.

Whatever they were doing with that portal needed to be stopped.

In the middle of the room, three other thieves fought off three guards who wore the blue museum uniform. Magic flashed from their hands, spikes of ice and flying jets of flame. But they kept the attack tight, contained. Their magic felt strong, like they could have blown the guards away.

But they held back. Did they want to avoid hurting the artifacts?

The guards rebuffed the attacks with circular shields. Magic repellers. When they could get a shot in, they sent blasts of golden light at the thieves.

Stunning spells, if I had to guess.

One crashed into the thief on the left, throwing him back almost to the portal.

"I'll take the guys on the left," I said.

"Right for me, then." Aidan threw a spear of flame, precise and blazing, toward one of the intruders. It engulfed him, and he fell to the floor, screaming.

I called upon Aidan's power over flame, using my Mirror Mage abilities to borrow his gift. It was safer than using my FireSoul power since Mirror Mages were accepted in magical society.

The evergreen scent of Aidan's magic filled my nose as I drew it into me and crafted a bolt of fire. Warmth filled me, that now-familiar joy, as I molded the magic to my will. I sent the fire streaking toward the thief who stood to the left of the portal.

Direct hit.

I grinned.

Flame licked up his form and he flailed, tumbling back into the portal and disappearing. A pang of loss hit me. If he hadn't fallen through the portal, I'd have been able to take his power.

"Oh, dear." Dr. Garriso's startled voice pulled me from my dark thoughts.

I flushed. What was I thinking?

I glanced toward Dr. Garriso. He'd entered through another exhibit and stood near the portal, his wide gaze traveling over the scene.

He was too near the last thief for my liking.

"Get back!" I shouted as I called upon Aidan's Elemental Mage powers and crafted a spear of ice. I'd wound the bad guy with this, then be able to question him.

The ice froze my fingertips as I sent it streaking through the air toward the final thief. It punctured him right through the middle. He flailed, knocking over an artifact case.

Dr. Garriso's shout echoed in the room. He lunged for the amphora that tumbled toward the floor. As he passed by the portal, it pulsed, a bright purple light illuminating the room. Magic surged, a dry static crackle in the air that made the hair on my arms stand on end.

The purple light expanded, reaching for Dr. Garriso and dragging him toward the heart of the portal. His wide gaze met mine as he was sucked inside. His sensible brown shoes were the last thing to disappear as I reached for him, my hand outstretched and too far away to be any help at all.

CHAPTER TWO

"No!" I lunged for Dr. Garriso, but he was long gone.

"Cass!" Aidan shouted as I sprinted for the portal.

Heavy footsteps thundered behind me. Just as I reached the glowing purple, an arm wrapped around my waist like a steel band and yanked me backward.

"You don't know what's on the other side." Aidan loomed over me, ten times as strong as I'd ever be. I suddenly wished I'd stolen that demon's immense strength back at P & P. Aidan could never have stopped me then.

I thrashed in his arms. "He's my friend!"

"I know, but we need to be—"

I stomped on his heel, dropped my weight, and thrust my elbow back into his gut. He *oofed* and let go of me. I threw myself at the pulsing purple light.

Pain.

I slammed into a wall. Stumbled back onto my ass. I blinked past the searing agony in my face and hands, which had hit the portal first. My face felt like it'd been stomped on by a giant troll.

Slowly, my gaze cleared. I was still in the museum. The portal pulsed with light, looking like it was open.

"The portal's closed." I struggled to my feet, my heart pounding desperately.

Aidan took my arm, his strong grip steadying me. "Damn it, Cass. That was stupid. Are you all right?"

"Don't worry about me." I pulled free and approached the portal. "We have to get to Dr. G! But why is the portal still here? It shouldn't be here if it's closed."

I reached out to the purple light. It glowed on my fingertips, turning them alien. A cold hardness met my touch.

"This is weird," I said. My skin chilled with fear-sweat, the worst kind. Dr. Garriso was *trapped*.

Aidan approached, extending his big hand and laying it next to mine. "No. This isn't right."

I turned to face the rest of the room. The guards were snapping pictures of the fallen bodies with their camera phones. No doubt in case they were demons and disappeared soon.

Good idea. I tugged my phone out of my pocket and went to the nearest man. He had pale skin and dark hair, and though I could see no horns, it didn't mean he wasn't a demon. Demons were the favored supernaturals to act as henchmen for the baddies in the magical world. I snapped a picture of him just as Aidan joined me.

Two of the guards approached, stopping in front of us. A burly one with dark hair and ruthlessly pressed clothes demanded, "Who are you? Why are you here?"

His tone pissed me off. "Uh, we just saved your ass."

"And threw the icicle that ended with Dr. Garriso sucked into that portal," he snapped.

That deflated me in a heartbeat. He was right. I was responsible. I'd been having such a good time with my magic, getting so cocky with my new skills, that I'd chosen a riskier magic because I'd wanted to question the thief. I should have recognized there were potential casualties in the room and used my lightning, but that was a FireSoul power. I didn't want these guards seeing it.

"I'm going to get him back," I said.

Aidan's hand gripped my own. Warmth filled my chest at the support.

"That doesn't answer my question. Who are you?" The ferocity in the guard's dark eyes cut me to ribbons.

"Friends of Dr. Garriso's," Aidan said. "We were in his office when we heard the fight."

"I didn't ask who you were to Dr. Garriso, I asked who you *were*," he barked.

Aidan grinned. "Well, why didn't you just say so? I'm Aidan Merrick."

The guard's gaze flew wide, startled. A gleam of sweat shined on his brow, the fastest flop-sweat I'd ever seen.

"Origin. I—I didn't realize."

I raised a brow. As far as I knew, only Shifters held that level of reverence for the most powerful of their kind. This guy was all Magica, though. It's not that Magica didn't respect Shifters, it was just that we were different. Magica *used* magic, whereas Shifters *were* magic. We were so different that we had our own governments and everything. The Order of the Magica ruled the magic users, and the Shifter Council ruled the Shifters.

Aidan nodded graciously at the guard, and I made a mental note to ask what the deal was. Was he a big donor at the museum or something? He *was* rich as twelve dragons.

The third guard entered the room, slipping a cellphone into his pocket as he walked.

"Administration is coming," he said. "Be here in five."

"Damn it!" The guard who'd interrogated us grimaced. "What the hell were those idiots thinking? You can't steal from here."

Which explained the guards' lackluster showing against the thieves. Magic ensured that nothing could leave the museum's walls, so the guards had gotten lazy. The protections were why I'd felt comfortable bringing the Chalice of Youth here for Dr. Garriso to look at before handing it over to Aidan for safekeeping. I hadn't anticipated this.

"What could they have been after in this room?" I asked.

The guard shrugged. "Same old stuff as in every other room."

"Old *stuff*? What are you, a troglodyte? This is our history! This *stuff* means something! It means a hell of a lot."

The guard stepped back, his hands raised. "Whoa, chill lady."

"Did you just tell me to *chill*? As in, calm down? When in the history of *ever* has that worked?"

He sputtered, but was cut off by the arrival of the museum administration. I didn't know what I'd expected—hadn't thought of it, really—but the people who walked in were far from the tweedy old nerds I'd imagined.

The two women and two men, all of them tall and thin and dressed entirely in black, looked like hawks. As they approached, their sharp eyes assessed the room, the shattered amphora that Dr. Garriso had tried to save, and the portal.

The head guard cleared his throat. "Madams and—"

The severest looking woman held up a thin hand. The guard's mouth snapped shut, and he appeared to wilt. The four approached the portal, their gazes darting around it. The sharp woman reached out to touch it. Her hand stopped, no doubt blocked as mine had been.

She turned, her gaze sweeping over the room. She wasn't my boss but even I felt a little anxious about her appraisal.

"They took nothing," she said.

"No, Madam Astrix," the guard said.

"But the portal remains. Why?"

"We don't know," the guard said.

"But it sucked in Dr. Garriso." I clenched my fists.

Her eyes widened. "How?"

My heart squeezed in my chest. *I* was at fault. Not that I'd admit it to her, though. "An amphora was falling off a table. He tried to save it and got too close to the portal."

She shook her head, her gaze grim. "Always thinking of history first."

"We have to get him out."

Madam Astrix nodded sharply. The three who stood partially behind her nodded as well, a mirror image of their leader.

"We will call the Order of the Magica. They will send investigators." She turned to the man on her left. "See that it's done."

He nodded and walked away. My heart thudded, threatening to break my ribs. investigators from the Order of the Magica? Sweat prickled my skin. The investigators were like the magical international super police—trained to carry out the Order's will and see to it that all laws were followed.

Like imprisoning FireSouls.

I'd never met an investigator before, and it'd sure as hell been on purpose. They were beyond qualified for their work, and I'd always been terrified they'd sniff me out.

Madam Astrix's eyes fell on Aidan. "Mr. Merrick. It is good to see you, but may I enquire as to why you are here?"

"We were seeing Dr. Garriso about an object when we heard the commotion from the break in."

"Thank you for intervening. They couldn't have stolen anything, but I'd hate to have seen anything else broken." Her gaze traveled around the room, landing on the shattered amphora. "Stupid thieves. Didn't they know it's impossible to steal from us?"

"It seems not," Aidan said. He glanced over his shoulder at the guard leaving the room, then turned back to her. "We will leave you to it."

"Again, thank you for your help," Madam Astrix said.

"Absolutely," Aidan said.

"And please let me know if there is anything we can do to help," I said.

"I'm sure the investigators will have it under control."

Maybe, but I wasn't about to be kept in the dark. As much as I wanted to stay the hell away from the investigators, it was my fault Dr. Garriso had fallen into the portal. I'd see to it he got out.

I was just about to ask for more information when Aidan gripped my arm and tugged gently, but determinedly. I suppressed my scowl and walked from the exhibit with him. As soon as we turned the corner and were out of Madam Astrix's eyesight, Aidan stopped, his posture alert. I could almost see his ears twitching.

"I assume we're not just leaving this alone, right? You know I need to make sure the Order of the Magica gets him back."

"Of course. The guard went left," he murmured, then set off that way.

I grinned, suddenly getting it.

"We're going to bribe him for info about the investigators, aren't we?" I asked as we strode through the nearly dark exhibit of ancient armor. The elaborate metal work gleamed dully in the minimal light.

"Absolutely," Aidan said.

"I like how you think."

"Likewise."

"And you make a good sidekick."

"Sidekick? I thought I was Batman and you were Robin?"

I punched him lightly. "Maybe. But then I get to be Wonder Woman."

We found the guard at the eastern exit, leaning against the wall outside, having a smoke. The rain had slowed to a drizzle, but the night was cool. The orange tip of his cigarette glowed in the dark. His annoyed gaze met ours. It wasn't the same angry guard, but rather the one who'd called administration.

"Yeah?" he said as we approached. His gaze widened when we stepped under the light. "Origin."

"Yes," Aidan said.

The man bowed low. I reached out for his power, getting a hint of animal musk and the sound of wind through the tress. A Shifter. Good. That'd make this easier.

"What can I do for you?" the guard asked.

"How'd you like to make a quick buck?" Aidan pulled a wad of cash out of an envelope.

He nodded eagerly. "To help you, sure. What do you need?"

"Let us know when the Order of the Magica arrives."

"All right." The guard's gaze was avid on the cash, then fearful on Aidan.

"And don't tell anyone we're interested," Aidan said.

"Of course."

"Excellent. And I'm sure you know what will happen if you don't stick to your agreement?" Aidan asked.

The guard swallowed hard and nodded.

"Good man." Aidan handed him the wad of cash. "My business card is there too. Call when you know something."

He nodded and we left, walking quickly through the dark night toward my car.

"That was smart," I said. "I want to come back and spy on the investigators."

"I thought you might. You've got good control of your magic signature, but it's not what it could be. You're fine around most other supernaturals by now, but no need to court trouble by meeting the investigators directly."

"And they wouldn't tell us anything useful. I'd rather have the information flowing from them to us rather than the other way around." But it warmed me that Aidan's first concern had been my safety.

Every supernatural gave off a magical signature—it could hit any of the five senses. Sometimes multiple. To me, Aidan's magic smelled like the forest, sounded like crashing waves, and tasted like chocolate. It took a strong supernatural to hide their signature. Though I was strong, I wasn't practiced.

I'd been hiding as a FireSoul so long that I'd only recently embraced using my magic. Though I'd learned to repress a lot of my signature, the investigators were trained to hunt my kind. It was way too risky to face them directly. My last run-in with a supernatural government—the Alpha Council—hadn't gone well. One of their own had discovered what I was. He was keeping my secret, but I couldn't count on the same leniency from the Order of the Magica investigators.

32

Aidan and I climbed into my old car. I turned the key, grateful to hear the engine crank to life.

"What if they weren't at the museum to steal something?" I asked as I navigated onto the street.

"I was wondering that," he said. "It's not exactly a secret that it's impossible to steal from the Museum of Magical History."

"Think they were after Dr. Garriso?"

"Could have been. He's a knowledgeable guy. Knowledge is powerful."

I clenched my hands on the steering wheel. If that was the case, I'd given him right over to them with my cockiness with the icicle. I sucked in a ragged breath.

"It's not your fault, Cass." Aidan gripped my thigh in a comforting squeeze.

How did he know so well what I was thinking?

Our arrival at Factory Row saved me from having to answer. I pulled my car into its usual spot along the street and turned the key.

"We're going to need a way to sneak up on the investigators," I said. "Let's see if Connor has anything to help us out."

Aidan's solemn gaze met mine, but I scrambled out before he could say anything. I wasn't going to be stupid and throw away whatever good thing I had with him by clamming up totally, but I didn't want to talk about my guilt right now. That would end up feeling like therapy, and I didn't have the time.

Aidan grabbed my hand as we crossed the street toward P & P. I squeezed, grateful for his presence. His patience.

Dark had fallen while we were driving home, and the windows of P & P glowed with warm yellow light. There were a couple patrons sitting at one of the many small tables, but it was the sight of my two *deirfiúr*, sitting in our favored comfy armchairs in the corner, that made me smile.

Del was back.

I hurried ahead, pushing through the door before Aidan could try something silly like holding it open for me.

I caught Connor's eye from behind the counter and nodded my head toward Del and Nix. A signal that I wanted to talk.

"Be there in a few," he said as he stirred a drink.

"Thanks." I glanced over at Aidan, who'd just entered.

"I'm going to see if Connor has any pasties in the back. Better to go back to the museum with some fuel in our stomachs."

"Thanks. Good thinking, but ask Bridget." I nodded toward the blond girl who sometimes worked the counter when Claire was on mercenary jobs. "I want to talk to Connor when he's free."

"Sure." He headed toward the counter, his tall form commanding the attention of the other patrons.

I turned to approach Del and Nix. "Del! You're back. You get your guy?"

"Better believe it." She grinned, her blue eyes sparkling. Her black hair was pulled back in a ponytail. "He put up a fight, but he's back in his hell now."

"Good." I flicked a hand over the sleeve of her black leather jacket. I favored brown, but Del was all about the black. "You got some blood there."

"Life of a demon slayer."

"Badass." I grinned, but everything that had happened recently wiped it off my face.

Del's eyes turned serious. "Nix told me about the two Tracker demons who came looking for us earlier today."

"Yeah. But we got them."

"The Monster had to have sent them," Del said.

My stomach turned at the mention of the shadowy man who haunted my memories and nightmares.

"Not for us necessarily," Nix whispered. She glanced at the other patrons, clearly trying to judge if they could hear us.

Fortunately, they got up to go, making their way to the exit, too slowly for my liking. When the door shut behind them, Nix turned back.

"The Monster is hunting FireSouls. All FireSouls. Some seer told him there are some here, but not us specifically. And our charms hide us."

"Yeah, that's true," I said. "But it's still no good if he's sniffing around."

"If he sends more scouts, we kill them. And if he doesn't know it's us who live here, he might give up and look for others."

"Maybe." The Monster was hunting FireSouls, enslaving them to use for unknown purposes. We didn't know what his end goal was, just that we didn't want to get caught.

Connor approached from the counter, a grin on his face. "What can I get you?"

Relieved, I turned to face him. "Not coffee. We need something a little more interesting."

Connor's dark brow quirked. "I'll have a seat, then. Claire's off on a job, but Bridget can watch the counter."

Connor sat as Aidan approached, a plate of pasties in his hand. My stomach grumbled at the smell of the savory treats. Claire and Conner were from Cornwall, in England, and had brought the Cornish Pasty, the most famous treat from their homeland, along with them. It was a specialty of the P & P. I had one in my mouth before the plate hit the little table in the center of our circle of chairs.

"Thanks," I mumbled around a bite of beef, potato, and flaky crust. Aidan always knew when to feed me. How had I gotten so lucky? And how had we not had time for more than a brief cuddle and kiss?

Connor tugged his chair closer and spoke softly. "What is it you need?"

Oh, right. That was why. Things were always chasing me or my friends lately. My life had been dangerous before, but ever since the Monster had reappeared a month ago, his agenda uncertain, things had been crazy.

I swallowed my mouthful and spoke. "We need something that will allow us to sneak up on someone. Like an invisibility potion or a glamour charm or something."

He nodded. "Invisibility potion, I can do. What do you need it for?"

I shrank in on myself a bit. I didn't mind admitting when I'd done wrong, but admitting to recklessness that had put a friend's life at risk was way harder than confessing to my normal blunders.

But I sucked in a deep breath and told them all about Dr. Garriso and what had happened at the museum with the errant icicle. I showed them the photo I'd taken of the fallen thief, but they didn't recognize his species. No surprise, really, since he looked human.

I finished by saying, "So we think they were possibly after him. And now we're just waiting for a call that'll tell us the investigators have arrived. I want to make sure they're doing a good enough job, and if they're not, we're going to do it for them. I can't just walk away from this."

"'Course not," Del said.

"A blocked portal, huh?" Nix said. "Never heard of one of those. Kinda goes against everything they're supposed to be."

"Yeah," Del said. "It's either a hole in space or it's not. A hole that leads nowhere isn't exactly a hole."

"Maybe it's a closed door," I said.

"That we can't open," Aidan said.

"Then we figure out how—"

Aidan's phone buzzed, cutting me off.

He pulled it from his pocket and stepped away.

Connor rose. "I'm going to go see what I can do about an invisibility potion."

"Thanks. You're the best."

Connor walked toward the back as Del leaned in and whispered, "How're you doing? Nix mentioned you had a little, uh, episode earlier with the demons who were looking for us."

An image of the white flame flickering across my skin flashed in my mind. The driving urge to steal the demon's power spiked within me, a ghostly memory. Nausea rolled in my belly. I'd almost stolen the one's power without even meaning to.

I glanced away, unable to look at Del. She and Nix had never had this problem. They'd resisted for years without effort. What made me so different?

"Uh, yeah. But it was nothing. I've got it under control."

"You sure?"

I cringed at the concern in Del's voice. "Yeah. If I didn't, I'd tell you."

And I would. Eventually. I just didn't want to talk about it now, so I reached for her hand and squeezed it. Nix's gaze met mine over Del's shoulder. The concern in Del's voice was mirrored in Nix's eyes.

Aidan returned. My shoulders relaxed. I didn't like having that kind of concerned attention. Praise and compliments, sure, but concern? Nope. I'd rather hang back along the sides while that was going around, thanks very much.

"Well?" I asked.

Aidan stopped before my chair, looming overhead. He was over six feet, a real bruiser of a guy. But that was one of the things I liked about him.

"The Order of the Magica investigators will be there in an hour to inspect the portal," he said.

"All right. Now we need a way back in."

"That won't be a problem. Origin Enterprises did an update on the Museum security a few years ago. I should be able to get us in."

"Good. Much easier than anything I'd have come up with." I grinned. "Is that why the security guards were so freaked out by you? And why Madam Astrix knew you?"

"No. Madam Astrix knows me because I'm a donor to their annual fundraiser."

As I'd thought. Richer than twelve dragons.

"And the security guards acted like cowards because I'm a scary bastard," he said.

Fair enough. I was no longer afraid of him, but I had been when I'd first met him. And whenever he turned into a griffin, his Shifter shape of choice, though I was getting over that.

"Great. I'm going to go check on Connor, see how he's coming with that invisibility potion."

I rose and wound my way through the small tables toward the counter at the back. Bridget was still mixing drinks—whiskey cocktails instead of coffee now that it was evening—and the breakfast treats tray in the glass case had been replaced with an assortment of savory pasties since they were more of a dinner item.

"I'm headed back to see Connor," I said to Bridget.

"All right." Her gaze stayed on the small bottle of bitters she was dashing into a glass of amber liquid.

I skirted around the counter and headed back through the swinging wooden door. The galley kitchen was small and cramped, but ruthlessly organized. I hurried to the door on the left and knocked. It was *not* smart to barge in on Connor when he was playing with his potions. Explosions, and all that.

Connor pulled the door open, wiping a hand on his band t-shirt. *Quartz*, this time. I'd never heard of them, but I assumed they were good, if Connor liked them. His dark hair flopped over his forehead.

"Hey. Almost got it done." He stepped back to let me in.

Though the coffee shop specialized in enchanted coffees, Connor liked to keep the potions themselves separate from the food. His workshop was slightly bigger than the kitchen, but far more cramped and cluttered. Rainbow vials of liquid crowded every shelf. Mortars and pestles and test tubes were scattered across the counter. It was a mad scientist's lair, all right.

Kitchen Connor was a dictator, potion Conner was an artist. He walked over to a small, smoking cauldron and gave it a stir.

"Won't taste good, but should do the job," he said.

"How long will it last?"

"An hour. Maybe a bit more."

I could work with that.

"But you'll have to keep control of your magical signature," he said. "It can't mask that."

My heart dropped. "Keep control? You mean, you've noticed it?"

"Only since you told me you're a FireSoul." He turned to meet me, his brown eyes kind. He was a couple years younger than my own twenty-five, but the kindness in his gaze was older. "I've been sensitive to it. Looking for it. But you're good at masking it. Only powerful supernaturals would notice it."

Like the investigators from the Order of the Magica. I swallowed hard, a chill prickling my skin.

"And only some of the time," he added. "Like I said, you're good at hiding it. It's not likely anyone will notice you, especially if they can't see you."

My shoulders relaxed a bit. He was right. They wouldn't be able to see me. And I'd thrown myself into practicing my magic—which made me a stronger Mage and better at hiding my signature overall—so I'd probably be okay.

Connor turned back to the cauldron and lifted it, pouring it into two small vials. After he corked them, he handed the vials over.

"These should do you. You'll be able to see each other because you drank the same potion, but no one else will."

"Thanks. What do I owe you?"

"Don't be dumb. Nothing. I like Dr. Garriso too." He made a shooing motion. "Now go get him back."

"Thanks." I gave him a quick hug and hurried out of the kitchen. I shoved the vials into the pocket of my leather jacket as I walked over to Aidan and my *deirfiúr*.

"Got it," I said. "Want to head over?"

"Sure."

"Need any help?" Del asked.

"Maybe, but not now. This is just recon, and we've only got enough potion for the two of us."

"Just let me know. I don't have another job for a couple of days. I'll just be scouring the archives for magic for you to hunt."

"Great. Thanks."

"Be safe," Nix said.

"Always." I turned and followed Aidan to the door, Nix's scoffing laughter following me out onto the street.

"What's her problem?" I grumbled.

"She sort of has a point," Aidan said as we crossed to Cecilia. "You do run at danger."

"It's part of my charm."

He grabbed my hand and squeezed. "It is, actually."

I smiled despite the rain that had picked up again, but thoughts of Dr. Garriso drove the grin from my face.

CHAPTER THREE

Aidan made the drive in record time. Now was not the moment to trust Cecilia to get the job done. We parked in the lot across from the museum, behind the old library that now served as a small local theatre.

I dug the vials out of my pocket and handed one over. "Here. It'll work for an hour. We'll still be able to see each other."

Aidan held the small bottle up to the dim light from the street lamp and squinted at the blue contents. "Bet it tastes like hell."

"Yep."

"Let's take it now. Won't take us long to get in, and we shouldn't risk being seen sneaking across the parking lot."

I held my vial up close to his. He clinked his against mine.

"Cheers," I said, then uncorked the bottle and poured it into my mouth.

A bitter, muddy taste flowed over my tongue. Vile. Magic rarely came without a cost. I choked it down.

Cold shivered along my limbs, followed quickly by a strange numbness. I flexed my fingers, staring at them. Would I be able to fight well like this? Numbness couldn't be good for the reflexes.

"Think it worked?" Aidan asked.

I scowled. He hadn't even grimaced. "I feel weird, so I guess so."

"Good enough. Let's go."

We climbed out of the car. I zipped my leather jacket against the rain and we sprinted across the gleaming street, then cut across the wet grass. Aidan led the way up the expansive stairs toward a tall window at the front of the building. Normally, I entered through the back basement, straight into the office wing to see Dr. Garriso. Aidan wanted us to waltz into the biggest exhibit hall in the place.

He stopped in front of the tall window and pulled a round metal charm out of his pocket.

"What's that?" I asked as he ran it around the edges of the window.

"Spell Stripper."

I sucked in a breath. "Holy magic, those are rare."

"Indeed. This one was made specifically for me. Only I can use it."

"So you can sneak back into the places you provide security for? Isn't that illegal?"

"I'm not all good, Cass."

Startled, I glanced up, meeting his dark eyes. The heart of him was there—the good Aidan I'd grown to trust—but so was the darkness that'd made me fear him when I'd first met him.

"But you're mostly good, right?" I asked.

He nodded. "Yeah, I think so. Where it counts."

I nodded. Considering that "where it counts" had been sticking by my side and saving me from nasty situations, I figured I could live with that. We all had a little darkness in us. Me, particularly, I was learning.

"Good enough for me," I said.

"Excellent." He returned the charm to his pocket and pushed open the window. "Shall we?"

"Wouldn't miss it." I hopped up onto the windowsill and climbed down into the huge atrium of the main entry hall.

No moonlight shined through the glass dome above, so the only light came from the dim recessed lights set into the walls. Shadows of statues and glass cases loomed in the darkness, places where anyone could hide.

Aidan landed silently next to me and shut the window, then ran the Spell Stripper over the edges again, presumably reigniting the protection spells.

"Let's go," he said.

We crept through the main part of the atrium, keeping our footsteps silent. My skin prickled to be so out in the open. Damn, I hoped these invisibility charms worked. I felt like I was just strolling through and could be spotted any moment.

I heard and saw no guards as we passed through a narrow room full of white marble statues. Ancient gods and goddesses draped in frozen fabric gazed impassively at us as we passed.

Like many museums, this one was a maze of different-sized rooms. Magic swelled from the room ahead of us, differing signatures that indicated the artifacts within were enchanted like the ones in my shop. Glass cases reflected the dim light. As soon as we stepped over the threshold, a ghostly howl broke through the silence.

It tore at my eardrums as the hair on my arms stood up. My gaze darted to Aidan's. Surprise flickered in his eyes.

Footsteps thundered toward us.

"Run," we said at the same time.

We retreated, sprinting back through the statue room and veering left down a narrow corridor lined with ancient shields. I tried my damnedest to keep my footsteps silent. Aidan, of course, had no problem with that, despite his great size. The Shifter in him gave him an unnatural grace.

Footsteps sounded behind us, but I didn't dare turn to look. I pushed myself faster, seeking a place to hide. We were invisible, but no need to court trouble. And I really didn't want to risk anyone sensing my magic.

We dove into a large exhibit of Egyptian statues. Towering Pharaohs loomed in the darkness. We ducked behind a sitting Hatshepsut, her throne giving us enough space to lean against her, side by side.

"What was that?" I panted, trying to keep my voice low. The ghostly howl was still screeching.

"Extra enchantments. That room had the most valuable stuff in the place. They must have doubled up on protection charms."

"Yeah, I felt the magic." I snapped my mouth shut when I heard footsteps.

I tensed, trying to calm my heart and hopefully any magic that I was putting out. As long as I didn't use it, I should be okay. Using magic was a bit like sweating. If you worked hard to access it, people would smell you. Or sense you, rather, depending on what kind of signature your magic gave off.

Aidan squeezed my hand as a guard walked in ten feet in front of us, his brow scrunched, like he sensed something was off here but couldn't figure it out. My heart pounded so hard I swore he could hear it. We could fight him if it came down to it, but then we'd lose any chance at eavesdropping on the investigators.

Finally, when I was about to start actually sweating, the guard turned and left. We sat in silence, each tense as boards, until Aidan finally relaxed.

"I heard them say it must have been a false trip," Aidan said.

"Thank god for Shifter senses." I didn't want to sit here too long, wasting our invisibility. "Come on, let's go."

We climbed to our feet and crept between the Egyptian statues, back down the hall, and around the room that had lost its shit at us. We took an alternate route, this one through an exhibit of daggers. My fingers itched to pocket one, but that was an obvious no-no.

I slowed my steps and my breathing as we neared the exhibit where Dr. Garriso had fallen through the portal. Aidan did the same. We nodded at each other, then slunk to either side of the entrance, each taking up a post and peering in.

The four administrators stood along the side of the room, watching the three investigators with sharp eyes. Two men and one woman, their magic radiating immense strength. Some supernaturals weren't afraid of showing off their power, though I could never understand why. There was an advantage in having people underestimate you.

The woman's power smelled like over-ripe apples. One man's magic felt like too-hot water against my skin, and the other's tasted like dirt. None of those were signatures I'd be showing off, despite their obvious power.

"It's strange," said the woman investigator. "I've never seen a portal like it."

She and the other two stood near it, peering intently into the pulsing purple light.

Had it gotten brighter? My skin prickled, a sickly wariness turning my stomach. Was that the portal? Was it giving off even more weird magic?

I focused on the investigators, trying to ignore the nerves that crept along my spine and keep my magic under control. It didn't take much, as long as I didn't actively use it, but I needed to be extra wary.

"And you say Dr. Garriso just fell through? And then it shut?" the taller male investigator asked.

"Yes," Madam Astrix said. "Though as it was described, he was sucked in."

"Hmmm. Portals don't do that," he said.

The woman investigator raised her hands. Silvery light flowed from her fingertips, disappearing inside the portal. She said, "And this is clearly a portal."

"It's residual at this point. Failed magic," the tall man said.

No. It didn't feel failed. Something was off about it.

"So you don't think it is anything more than a portal created by stupid thieves intent on stealing from a place that cannot be stolen from?" Madam Astrix asked.

"While that is possible, I doubt it," the woman investigator said. "But we will retrieve Dr. Garriso. We'll have to call in a Transporter to see if they can get through the barrier. In scenarios like this, their unique power helps them cross the closed portal."

"Excellent. When can we expect them?" Madam Astrix's worried gaze darted to the portal. "Dr. Garriso is not used to such hardship. He is a scholar."

That was the truth. He had a brilliant mind and a cunning wit, and I'd no doubt he could handle himself in a fight, but only if it were an even fight. And you couldn't count on even fights in this world.

"It shouldn't be more than twenty-four to thirty-six hours," the tall man said. "We'll call in a transporter, but we only have two and both are on jobs right now. But they will come right away."

I had to stifle a growl as my skin heated. A whole day? Maybe more?

"Is there nothing else you can do?" Madam Astrix frowned.

"Not at the present, though we can send our findings back to the Order and see what they have to say. We'll also stay and monitor it for changes. It should close on its own as the magic fades. A week, maybe a bit longer. I've seen the like before."

This was such bull.

The female investigator stiffened, her head jerking toward me. She sniffed, her nostrils flaring.

"Who's there?" she demanded.

Shit.

The heat on my skin wasn't just anger. It was the invisibility charm fading. We were near the end of our hour. She'd be able to see us any second. I met Aidan's gaze. He was thinking the same thing.

"The lights," I mouthed. I wanted the cover of darkness as we fled back into the museum.

He nodded.

My magic reached out for his, calling for his Elemental Mage powers and finding the chill of ice. I breathed deeply as I embraced it, cold air in my lungs, and tried to control my power so they wouldn't sense me. I raised my hand and threw tiny bullets of ice at the lights in the ceiling, small enough I hoped they wouldn't see them.

They raced through the air, tiny pinpricks of ice, and shattered the bulbs.

I grinned. Damn, I was getting good at this.

Aidan did the same, blowing out the rest of the lights.

Darkness crashed. The investigators and administrators shouted, but I didn't stick around to hear. I spun and raced into the darkened museum, my back now protected, Aidan at my side.

My breath heaved and lungs ached as I pushed myself faster, praying they wouldn't get to a light and see my hair. The red was pretty distinct. Not to mention, Aidan wasn't a subtle guy.

We streaked for cover along the wall, racing behind the looming statues toward the narrower hallway I knew lay at the other end. Footsteps pounded behind us as we darted into the dark hall.

Aidan spun and flung out his hands, sending a streak of power at the hall entrance. A thick wall of ice formed, glittery and blue even in the dark.

"That should take them a second," he said. "But no time to waste."

"Agreed."

We turned and sprinted down the hall. Shouts sounded on the other side of the makeshift wall. As we neared the door at the end, I called upon my Mirror Mage power and accessed Aidan's gift of the wind. It filled me, a cool breeze that brought joy in its wake. A torrent gusted from my fingertips and blew the door outward, breaking whatever lock had kept it closed.

"Nice one," Aidan said as we sprinted into the dark night. "I hardly sensed your magic at all."

"Thanks—" I panted, too exhausted to do anything but run. We raced across the grass and around the old library, then dove into Aidan's car.

"Take the back way." I dragged the seatbelt on.

"Not my first rodeo."

I laughed and wheezed at the same time, peering over my shoulder to see if anyone was coming.

No one.

I leaned back against the seat, gulping air. "I really need to work on my cardio."

Aidan laughed, his breathing short as well, and drove us away from the museum.

"What bastards," I said as we passed through the business district. It'd taken me two neighborhoods to catch my breath. "Waiting a whole day?"

"Not everyone has a Transporter on hand."

"No." I reached toward the communication charm that hung around my neck. "But I do."

I pressed on the silver pendant to turn it on. Comms charms were basically magical cellphones. Though I had a cellphone, I preferred this. No roaming charges.

"Del?" I said.

A moment later, her voice came through, along with what sounded like a fight. "Cass? What's up?"

"I need your help."

"Sure. I'm still dressed for business."

Which meant leather instead of pj's, if I knew Del. She had two modes: full throttle and couch.

"Can you meet me at my place?"

"Sure"—the sound of a scuffle interrupted—"stay down, you bastard!"

"You busy?"

"Just finishing an impromptu job." A pained grunt echoed though the comms charm. Sounded masculine, so likely not Del's. When she said she was still dressed for business, I guess she meant she was still *doing* business.

"Be safe," I said.

"Almost done. Meet you at your place in thirty."

"Thanks. Good luck."

I pressed the charm again to turn it off. A few minutes later, we pulled back onto Factory Row. P & P was hopping, more of the late-night crowd having shown up for Connor's fancy cocktails. Laughter echoed across the street as the door opened and someone ducked inside the party.

Aidan parked, and I jumped out and crossed the street to the green door beside Ancient Magic. I ran my hands along the edges to unlock the protection spells, then pushed the door open as Aidan joined me. He followed me up the three flights of stairs, past Nix's place on the first floor and Del's on the second, until we reached my landing. In addition to the shop on the bottom floor, we rented the whole top three floors of the building, over twelve thousand square feet combined. One floor for each of us.

I pushed open the door to my tiny apartment. About fifteen percent of my floor was living space, and what there was was crappy. But it was home. The good part, my trove, was hidden behind a secret door in my bedroom. That was where my priorities lay and my paycheck went.

The quiet of my apartment crashed around me. It'd been so go-go-go since this afternoon that nothing had had a chance to hit me. And the familiarity of this place—the battered furniture, the faded wallpaper, the empty PBR can on the coffee table—made me think how much about myself was no longer familiar.

Suddenly, I was exhausted. I sat on the couch and tried to keep the sigh from heaving out of me. "We'll wait for Del here."

Aidan joined me. "Hey, what's wrong?"

"Nothing. Just worried about Dr. Garriso." Wearily, I scrubbed a hand over my face. "And it's getting late."

Aidan tugged me against his side, and I melted into him. "I believe both of those statements, but there's a hell of a lot more you're not telling me."

"Yeah?"

"Yeah. You've got to trust me, Cass. I want more than just a date with you—which it looks like we'll never get a chance to have—so we're going to have to start sharing our dark secrets without it."

"Didn't we already do that?" We'd had a pretty good heart-to-heart last week.

"No, we told each other about our tragic Lifetime-TV-movie-childhoods. I'm talking about whatever it is that made you not call me back while I was away and whatever this guilt is that you're feeling over Dr. Garriso."

"Shouldn't I feel guilty? I got cocky with my magic and was reckless. I should've gone for something different. Fire. Lightning."

"There's no way to know what would have worked better. And I think you're reaching with the guilt."

"I just feel so out of control now. My magic is getting better, and I love it. Like, *really* love it. But I've been changing." I reached for the dagger strapped to my thigh and fiddled with it, a nervous habit. "It's like using my magic ignited the FireSoul part of me that I've been ignoring. And now that it's awake, I don't like what I'm finding."

"What do you mean?"

My mind flashed back to a week ago, when I'd last killed and stolen another supernatural's magic. Sickness twisted my insides. "I didn't tell you what happened when I stole the Shifter's power back in Turkey."

"Then tell me now."

"It's like something came over me. This enormous hunger to take her power. Like an addiction. It's not that I have a problem stealing powers from bad people—I can use it to fight the Monster that hunts me—but it's the fact that I was compelled to do it. And that I *liked* doing it. Shouldn't that be wrong? Shouldn't I be more in control?"

"I don't know." He squeezed my shoulder. "But I do know that power can be addictive. It's basic. It's survival. It's hard to fight that kind of pull when you have access to it."

I glanced up at him. His jaw was set, and he stared toward the door.

"Sounds like you know something about it," I said.

"Yeah, a bit." He reached up and rubbed a hand over his face. "The Origin has a lot of power. But it can twist a person. I told you about my father."

I nodded. Madness ran in his family, spurred on by the immense amount of power that the Origins possessed. Aidan's dad had ended up killing two other Alpha Council members. Aidan had had a rough childhood with a murderer for a father.

"But it's not just that. There's something more basic to the pursuit of power. At least, the kind I think you're dealing with. When I first started shifting into a griffin, it was this enormous surge of power. I was the strongest mythical creature—besides dragons, which no one can shift into—and could terrify or kill whatever I wanted. The griffin knew this. When I shifted, I wasn't entirely myself. The griffin held the reins too. Like your FireSoul. The magic part and the human part trying to live in harmony. It took me a long time to get it under control."

I shivered, the image of Aidan in his griffin form sharp in my mind. He was terrifying in that form, though beautiful. "So I was right to be afraid of you in your griffin form."

"Not anymore. The griffin urges are still there, but I've banked them so far down that I'm in control now. You will be too."

"How?"

"Practice."

"Always practice."

"Always. But it means the urge to take other supernaturals' magic isn't really your fault. It's the FireSoul in you. Part of you, but not all you."

"But what if it takes over? Makes me try to steal good people's powers?" I didn't say the worst part. That to steal them, I'd have to kill. That was my biggest fear. Killing when I didn't have to, just to take the power.

He reached an arm around me and squeezed me to his side. "You won't. You'll fight it. The power is seductive, but you'll find your way to the other side."

I hugged him, breathing in his forest scent. "How'd you get to be so smart?"

"I've got a few years on you."

"Not that many."

"Then I'm just a genius."

I grinned up at him, then raised my head to kiss him. A knock sounded at the door.

"We really need to find a few minutes when we're not running for our lives or someone else's," I muttered. "Because we cannot catch a break."

"Agreed." The heat in his gaze burned me.

Reluctantly, I pulled out of Aidan's arms and stood. "Come on in, Del!"

The door opened, and Del stepped through. Her black hair was pulled back in a ponytail, and her blue eyes stood out starkly in her pale face. More blood splattered her black leather jacket, visible only by its gleam and my keen eye.

"Thanks for coming so quickly," I said. "Finish beating up whatever demon you caught?"

"Yeah. That's what I get for thinking I was on a break. Claire needed help with a particularly iffy job, so I volunteered."

"Ready to volunteer again?"

"Born ready." She waggled her eyebrows.

I laughed at the awful joke, punch-drunk from exhaustion. I'd been in how many fights or run-for-my-life situations today? I was going to need to sleep for a week when this was over.

"So what do you need?" Del asked as she sat in the chair by the window.

The memory of our task sent Dr. Garriso's face into my mind's eye. Worry followed. I paced in tight little lines as I told her about the investigators and the portal. "So I need you to take me through. Tonight. The Magica are too slow. We can't leave Dr. Garriso there for another day."

"Agreed. Shall we get Nix?"

"Yes. More help, the better."

"My thoughts exactly." Del stood. "Lead the way."

"Thanks." I'd never doubted she would do it. "Now we need a plan to get past the Magica."

CHAPTER FOUR

Getting past the Magica turned out to be easier than I'd expected. Connor had just enough ingredients left to make invisibility potion for the four of us, and Del transported us straight to the portal entrance. It was a short distance from Factory Row, so it wasn't a big drain on her transportation magic. She'd still be able to get us through the portal and back out, thank magic. I really hadn't wanted to sneak through the museum again.

Once had been enough for me, thanks.

When we appeared in front of the portal, all of my muscles tensed. The two guards leaned against the wall, their gazes on the portal, and one of the Magica investigators stood by the entrance, a phone pressed to his ear.

The air felt strange, as if it were thicker. I shook it off. Probably getting paranoid. Being invisible wasn't as fun as I'd expected.

None of them looked our way. My shoulders relaxed slightly. Thank magic for Connor's skill with a cauldron. I turned back to Del. The portal glowed purple on her face as she reached out to touch it. Her hand stopped just before passing through.

Still closed.

She nodded and reached out for our hands. I clasped hers and Nix gripped her other. Aidan's hand folded around mine. A second later, I felt the familiar pull of the ether.

Within the space of a breath, we appeared on the other side. The air was hot and humid, then dry and cold, flashing back and forth. We stood in a desert, golden sand stretching out around us. Then the vision wavered.

Suddenly, we were standing in a jungle, green foliage spread out around us and animals screeched in the distance. Enormous leaves rustled overhead and the jungle air felt like hot soup. The ground was spongy beneath my feet. But none of it looked quite solid or real. At times I thought I heard laughter or voices, as if there were people nearby. Then it was gone.

A second later, we were standing in an abandoned city. Cold wind whipped through the empty streets. Skyscrapers soared toward a sunless sky, and eerie quiet descended. Paper blew across the street in front of us, and an old brown sedan sat forsaken. It looked like a movie about the apocalypse.

But worse, the feel of dark magic washed over me, a horrible prickly sensation. My stomach turned.

"The Monster," I whispered.

Del's hand tightened in mine. "I feel it."

"This is his place," Nix said as the scenery around us wavered, turning back to desert and then to an icy hellscape. The snow glittered white under the light of a non-existent sun.

Where the hell was the light even coming from?

"What is it?" Aidan asked.

"I have no idea." I shuddered, the cold streaking through me. "It's not real and it's not anywhere on Earth. This magic is too strange. Too strong."

"I think it's a waypoint between Earth and the heavens and hells," Del said. "I've read about these places. Nothing is stable or solid."

"Oh, great. So we're not on Earth." That had never been on my travel itinerary before. For good reason. "Let's find Dr. Garriso and get the hell out of here."

My skin still prickled with unease, an undeniable sense that the Monster was near. Whispers teased at my ears, snippets of conversation I couldn't quite grasp. As if there were people in a room just next door.

I tried to force my heartbeat to calm and closed my eyes, focusing on Dr. Garriso. I called forth my dragon sense to find him, filling my mind with images of his face and everything I held dear about him.

His support, his conversation, his knowledge.

The familiar sense of direction tugged at my middle, pulling me left. Relief filled me, a balm that drove away some of the horrible prickly feeling of this place. I wouldn't be able to find him if he weren't alive.

I pointed. "That way."

My boots crunched in the ice as we set off. My leather jacket did me no good. My skin was so cold it almost burned.

"Fake Antarctica was not where I expected to end up," Nix said.

We'd dragged Nix away from a Netflix marathon, but as always, she'd come willingly.

"That's the truth." Our surroundings wavered. I squinted, trying to make out what world we'd be walking into next.

Noise and heat crashed around me. Blazing sun beat down, nearly blinding. I blinked, desperately trying to regain my vision. We were in an enormous stadium.

No, a coliseum. People dressed in Roman togas screamed and waved their fists at the gladiators below. Dust billowed beneath the fighters' feet as they danced around each other, swords clashing.

Did this waypoint take us between times as well as worlds?

Toga-clad people turned to point and shout at us.

"We need to get out of here," Aidan said.

"Agreed," Del said. "I don't want to be burned as a witch for appearing out of the blue."

I nodded vehemently, though I wasn't sure if the Romans burned people as witches. It didn't really matter, though. Anyone capable of appearing out of thin air probably looked dangerous and in need of serious questioning.

"Come on!" Aidan said, then turned and pushed his way through the crowd toward the nearby stairs. We followed him, single file, taking advantage of the path he'd created and sprinting down the stone steps.

More and more people turned to look at us instead of the battle below. Our clothes were so strange. Pants in ancient Rome? Talk about weird. I couldn't sense any magic, which meant we were likely among mortals. A few mortals were no problem. But this many mortals?

A *big* problem. I didn't want us getting caught in some sticky situation that necessitated Del transporting us out of here. She needed to save her power for the return journey to Magic's Bend.

Heavily armed men blocked our exit at the bottom of the stairs, their swords raised and glinting in the light.

"No magic!" I hissed at my companions. "They're human!"

I reached for my daggers, hesitating when the scene began to waver. The gladiators and sunlight disappeared, replaced by darkness, strobe lights, and pulsing music.

"What the hell!" Nix shouted from beside me.

All around us, hundreds of bodies danced to the techno music that blared from enormous speakers set upon a raised stage. Rainbow-colored strobe lights lit the scene. Magic flowed from the inhabitants, a cacophonous blend of scents, tastes, feelings.

We were in some kind of supernatural dance club, likely in an all-magic city somewhere in Europe.

"I take it back!" Nix said. "I think I prefer fake Antarctica!"

So did I. It was damned hard to follow my dragon sense with so much going on around me. I had to close my eyes to focus on it. But it was elusive, the feel of Dr. Garriso's location only a weak tug about my middle. Left? Forward?

Finally, I picked up the thread of it and followed the tug, turning around and pointing toward the main part of the club. The dance floor was huge, an endless sea of supernaturals of all shapes and sizes. Even demons danced, their weird shapes and colors standing out amongst the more human-looking supernaturals.

"There!" I pointed. "The exit past the dance floor."

I stepped aside to let Aidan lead, figuring his bulk was better to part the crowd. It worked, and we followed him through the writhing bodies. I slapped a hand that reached for my ass, but by the second one, I was pissed. That guy got a punch straight to the nose.

"Bitch!" he cried, then grunted.

I turned to see him doubled over and Nix shaking her fist.

"Moron!" she yelled, then turned and winked at me.

We pushed our way through the crowd to catch up to Aidan, who'd stopped in the middle of the crowd to wait for us. A trio of Barbie dolls had turned to stare appreciatively at him. They were approaching when I reached him. I hissed—honest to god, *hissed*—which was really embarrassing, but they backed off.

Apparently I was territorial around Aidan. That was new for me, but now was hardly the time to examine it.

Actually, *never* was the time to examine it.

We set off through the crowd again, following in Aidan's wake. The exit light beckoned. What city would we step out into?

The ground fell out from under me. A scream strangled in my throat as I clawed at the air. I crashed into icy cold saltwater. It blinded me, filling my mouth and cutting off my scream. I kicked for the surface, praying it was near.

When my head broke through, I searched for Aidan and my *deirfiúr*. Nix broke the surface first, followed by Aidan, and finally Del.

"What the hell!" Del sputtered.

I choked on salt water as I spun in a circle, searching for land. Great cliffs soared in the distance, red stone dully reflecting the light of a sun I couldn't see.

"Hang on," Nix said. She raised her hands above the water. Blue light glowed around them, and her brow scrunched in concentration. A moment later, a small rowboat appeared.

Thank magic for her ability to conjure.

We swam for the boat, scrambling in and collapsing against the sides. I panted, exhausted, my eyes burning from the seawater. Everyone looked like drowned rats, their hair plastered to their heads. I looked no better, I was sure.

"Damn, this sucks," I said.

"I gotta say, I wasn't expecting the ocean," Aidan said.

"Does this mean there could be lava?" Nix asked.

"For magic's sake, I hope not." I focused on my dragon sense again, grateful to find that it pulled us towards land. "Dr. Garriso is on that piece of land."

"Thank God he's not in the water," Nix said. "I can't imagine he's a strong swimmer."

"You'd be surprised," I said. "Dr. Garriso looks fragile, but he's tough."

Nix conjured two oars and passed them over to Aidan. "Here you go, big guy. Put those muscles to use.

Assuming we don't end up in a volcano with the next world shift, I'll take over in a bit."

Aidan nodded and took the oars, then slotted them into the oarlocks and began to row. Waves crashed against the boat, sending us rocking. Cold water splashed. I shivered and huddled deeper into my now-soaked jacket. I debated using magic to dry myself, but decided to save it.

"Only a few hundred more yards!" Del called from her place at the bow. Land beckoned.

The water around us turned to sand.

The boat stopped dead.

Dry heat filled my lungs.

Desert again.

"At least our clothes will dry quick," Nix said.

We climbed out of the boat and set off, used to the crazy changes by now.

"How far did Dr. Garriso go?" As soon as I asked the question, I caught sight of a collapsed figure a hundred yards away. The dark clothes stood out starkly against the golden sand.

My heart pounded. I ran ahead, pushing myself as the sand dragged at my boots. It was Dr. Garriso. It had to be. When I neared, I could make out his white hair and tweed coat.

The tightness in my chest loosened. He was going to be all right.

Suddenly, stone walls crashed down around me, cutting out the light. A torch crackled in its wall sconce, throwing a small amount of light into the room. I stumbled on the stone ground that was suddenly beneath my feet. Dr. Garriso lay ahead, but when I whirled, all I saw were stone walls. Not even a door.

Nix, Del, and Aidan were gone.

And I was in a cell.

My heart beat frantically, and sweat broke out on my skin. "What the hell."

Dr. Garriso didn't answer. I fell to my knees beside him, wincing at the hard stone.

Gently, I shook his shoulder. "Dr. Garriso. Wake up. We have to get out of here."

How, I had no idea.

Dr. Garriso's face was slack, his breathing slow. Passed out. Or magically subdued? I couldn't tell which.

Panic beat its fists against my ribs as I climbed to my feet and went to a wall. I pounded against the stone. All it did was make my hands sore.

I swallowed hard, shaking. This wasn't like the rest of the world changes. It felt more deliberate.

I turned to face the room.

A door appeared in the wall.

Shit.

Suddenly, this was all too familiar. Like the cell I'd been locked up in as a child.

A tall, slender figure walked through. He was dressed entirely in black—appropriate for this creepy place—and his skin was so pale he was almost transparent. Even his hair was nearly see-through. Though this whole area vibrated with the Monster's evil magic, this man wasn't the Monster.

"Who are you?" I demanded. "Where am I?"

I reached out for his power, seeking his signature to get a better feel. When the smell of magic hit me—smoke and burning—I stumbled back into the wall.

"Holy magic, you're a FireSoul."

"Indeed." His voice was as crisp and cold as a winter morning.

In a place that reeked of the Monster's dark magic? "What is this place? Why are you here? Where are my friends?"

He swept his pale hands out in front of him. "It is my creation."

"The whole waypoint?"

He laughed, a horrible sound that sent a shiver down my spine. "Would that it were. No, just this dungeon."

"You built it quick."

"I'm powerful."

I could feel that. His power vibrated on the air. It smelled like burning plastic and felt like a cold trickle down my spine.

"But this place smells like the magic of a man I know. And you aren't him." It made my stomach turn to call him a man.

"No, that I am not. But I am his."

The hair on my arms stood on end. If he worked for the Monster, I couldn't let him take me or my *deirfiúr*. But questions burned my tongue.

"You're not wearing a collar," I said, thinking of the collar that Aaron had worn. Aaron had been a FireSoul slave of the Monster's. I'd met him once not long ago and killed him, though I hadn't wanted to.

"It is unnecessary." He approached, his walk so graceful that he almost glided. "I am willingly his."

I stepped back. "His creature, you mean? Minion to a monster?"

He shrugged. "Monster, genius."

"Why would you side with someone like him? After all he's done?" Enslaving child FireSouls, murder, torture.

He looked at me like I was stupid and said, "Power."

Power. Obviously.

"The magic he has taught me is like none you'll ever know."

"And I don't want to know."

"Don't you, FireSoul? I can sense your power. Sense that you've killed for it." He roamed the edge of the room, a spider drawing close to its prey.

"I had to," I said.

"Not true."

No, it wasn't. And that reality scared me.

"And you liked it," he said.

I shook my head, though he was right. I liked not just the power, but the act of stealing it. But I didn't want to like it. It was a fine line to walk—managing the power without becoming consumed.

This man was consumed.

There was so much that I wanted to ask, but it was past time for me to be getting out of here. This world was the Monster's, and this guy couldn't be here for anything good.

I steadied myself, calling upon my magic and reaching out for his. I needed to know what I was up against if I was going to fight him. His magic felt strange and subtle, unlike most. Elemental mage powers hit you in the face normally, and so did most of the others. But this was odd.

Finally, I grasped it.

He was an Illusionist. The most powerful I'd ever met if he could make his illusions as real as the stone that had bruised my fists.

Awkwardly, I pulled his magic toward myself, struggling to manipulate it into something I could use. I'd never mirrored an Illusionist before.

I went for something easy, creating a shimmery illusion of smoke that surrounded him, obscuring Dr. Garriso and myself at the edge of the room. I lunged left, then called upon my lightning, letting it fill me with a crackling burn.

Thunder boomed and the bolt streaked toward him. But it passed through him, then streaked through the rock wall behind him.

Both were illusions.

Shit.

An arm wrapped around my neck from behind, a steel bar that cut off my breath. I thrashed.

"Using my own powers against me?" he hissed. "Mirror Mage, are you?"

So he didn't know what I was? Or who?

This close, I couldn't use lightning or risk frying myself too. I grabbed for the dagger strapped to my thigh, but before I reached it, iron manacles snapped around my wrists. He grabbed my arm and yanked it back, trapping my hands near my waist.

Too far from my blades.

Shit.

I struggled, but he was stronger than he looked.

"Not so fast," he said.

I kicked back, nailing him in the shin. He grunted, then stood and tugged me up. I dropped my weight, hoping to break his hold, but he just dragged me away from Dr. Garriso's body.

"Where the hell are you taking me? You're just going to leave him there?"

"Don't need him. But the master might like you. Another FireSoul. Knew it as soon as I felt you."

Oh, hell no.

I called upon my lightning, doing my damnedest to keep it minimal, and sent a bolt into his middle. A horrible noise escaped his throat as he collapsed. It shocked me, too, sending painful electricity through my limbs. Nothing like actually using the magic.

I scrambled across the stone toward his body, my limbs weak as jello. With a shaking hand, I reached for the dagger strapped to my right thigh. The dungeon still surrounded us, so he wasn't incapacitated enough for his magic to fail.

He surged up, a silver knife in his hand and rage in his eyes. He looked mad enough to kill me. I lunged for him, my blade glinting black in the dim light.

But he reached me first, sinking his dagger into my arm. Agony bloomed hot and fierce as warm blood poured down my arm. I forced myself to tighten my grip on my blade and heaved myself against him, throwing him onto his back.

I plunged my dagger down, satisfaction arcing through me when it sank easily into his chest. He struggled weakly, his dark eyes dimming. I'd hit him straight in the heart, a quick death.

As soon as his blood welled, the familiar hunger arose, clawing at me. My FireSoul roared up, ravenous, and white flame flickered across my skin, reaching out for his magic. I ached for it, for the moment his power would flow into me. It'd be so good. So, so good.

No.

I reared back, sucking in a ragged breath. His struggles slowed, enticing the FireSoul within me even more. My hands burned to push him down, suck out his power, and make it mine.

That wasn't me. I didn't want it to be me.

I had to control it. I had to fight this.

But it called to me. Not just the hunger—the power itself. This man's magic, his power over illusion, was one of the greatest magical gifts I'd ever seen. It'd be such an incredible weapon against the Monster.

Though the emptiness roared within me, I clung to that rational thought. To any rational thought. This was too great a gift to leave behind. But I had to be in control if I were going to take it.

Deliberately, I pressed my hands to his shoulders, trying to control the process of taking his magic. Trying not to let it overcome me. I didn't want to become the ravenous thing that I feared my FireSoul would make me. The man below me was proof of what the desire for power could do.

I had to be present for this act—me controlling my FireSoul, not the other way around.

The white flame licked over my arms, bright and fast, and reached into him. It burned, but I embraced the pain as payment for the deed I was about to commit.

When my magic latched on to his, I almost retched. It felt dark, tainted. But after a moment, the sickness faded. As he died, I realized his magic had been tainted by his evil. When I drew it back into myself, it was pure. Bright and sparkling like champagne.

Warmth and strength surged as it flowed into me. It was both wonderful and uncomfortable, a pleasure I shouldn't be taking as a result of theft, but I couldn't help myself.

When it ended, I fell off of him. He stared at the sunless sky, his gaze blank.

Thank magic, the illusion of the dungeon had faded. I was back in the desert.

"Cass!" Aidan roared.

I scrambled to my feet and spun to face him.

He, Del, and Nix raced across the sand toward me. Thank magic they were safe. I turned and crawled across the sand toward Dr. Garriso, my limbs still trembly.

I knelt over him, pressing my fingers to his throat and staring fixedly at his chest. It rose beneath the tweed coat. My shoulders slumped. He still breathed.

"Are you all right?" Del fell to her knees beside me.

"Fine."

"We could feel you," Nix said. "But we couldn't get to you."

Aidan swooped me up in his arms. Hugged me. Pain streaked through my arm. My wound. I cried out.

"Shit. Sorry." Aidan loosened his grip and set me on my feet. His concerned gaze raced over me, settling on my arm. "Are you all right?"

"Yeah." I tugged my jacket off and winced at the size of the slice in my bicep.

Nix tugged the thin linen scarf from around her neck and tied it over the wound. I flinched, but at least the blood flow would lessen.

"Let me heal you," Aidan said.

"No, we need to get out of here. Now. This is connected to the Monster somehow."

Nix's and Del's stark gazes met mine.

"I knew it." Nix shook her head.

"Can you carry Dr. Garriso?" I asked Aidan. "Del, can you take us back?"

"Yeah, let's get out of here. I can't transport to the waypoint—I need to save my power to get across, back to earth. But if we can make it to the portal, I can get us across, into the museum. Once we're on Earth, hopefully I'll have enough power to get us where we need to go, but no guarantees."

Aidan picked up Dr. Garriso. "To the hospital in Magic's Bend."

"Okay," Del said. "Let's go, then. I'll lead the way."

I sucked in a ragged breath of hot desert air. Pain blazed in my arm, and I felt like I'd run a marathon. Trekking across this sand was not my idea of a good time. I was just grateful that Del was using her dragon sense to find the portal. I didn't have the energy.

"Right," Del said, and set off.

We followed, Aidan carrying Dr. Garriso and me leaning on Nix. We dragged ourselves across the sand, down a mountain, over a moor, and through a jungle. I hated this damned place.

"You okay?" Nix asked.

I thought of the power I'd stolen, of how I'd been more in control this time. "Yeah, I think I'm doing all right."

And I meant it. Maybe I could get a handle on this whole FireSoul thing.

"Good. We were scared."

"Me too." Fates, I was tired.

Finally, the purple glow of the portal appeared on the horizon. If we hadn't had a FireSoul's ability to find what we sought, we'd have been screwed. The changing scenery did not lend itself to navigation, and I seriously doubted a compass would work. Not that I knew how to use one. Never needed to learn.

We reached the glowing purple portal and clustered around Del, each making contact.

A second later, we stood in the museum.

"Oh, shit," I said.

The room blazed purple. The air was thick as soup. And the guards and investigator were frozen in place, their bodies like mannequins, expressions of horror etched on their faces.

CHAPTER FIVE

"Get us out of here, Del." Aidan's voice sounded slow.

I reached for Del, my arm moving so sluggishly it was like I was dragging it through sand. The air was thick, viscous. I moved slower with every millisecond that passed, like I was freezing in place with the portal.

The faces around me glowed in the purple light, which pulsed behind us. The sickening feeling of the Monster's magic surged from it.

I could feel Del struggle to access her power. Her magic swelled, feeling like soft grass beneath my feet and smelling like fresh laundry, but it faltered, less sure than normal.

Finally, we began to disappear. But even that happened slowly, as if the portal were loath to let us go. It had trapped the guards and investigator and was trying to trap us too. Normally, transporting blinked you out of a place so quickly you didn't realize it.

This time, I watched as my *deirfiúr* faded. It was eerie as hell.

What felt like ages later, we found ourselves standing in the lobby of the town hospital. Bright white linoleum and the smell of antiseptic dragged me back to reality.

My arm started hurting. Worry for Dr. Garriso swelled.

A nursed rushed from behind the counter, her eyes wide.

"This way!" She gestured, leading us through swinging gray doors and into a wide hallway.

Everything else happened in a blur. The healers took Dr. Garriso away on a stretcher, and I was moved to a regular healer's exam room. Medical implements and magical potions were scattered on the shelves. Magical medicine was a bit like human medicine, from what I'd seen on television. Some things were treated with human means, others with magic. Most with magic, though a good band-aid was never turned down.

Aidan stood by my side. Del and Nix had gone with Dr. Garriso.

"How are you doing?" he asked as he stepped around to my wounded arm.

"Great." My arm burned, blood dripped onto the floor, and the rest of me felt like I'd been hit by a dump truck. "Remind me how many fights I've been in today? Three? Four? I think I'm losing it."

He leaned down and kissed my forehead. "You deserve a nap. But first, let me see if I can do something about this arm. At least make it feel better before the real healer comes in to finish the job."

Aidan hovered his palm over the wound beneath Del's scarf. Warmth flowed through my arm, bringing with it relief.

I plopped my head against his chest. "That feels so much better."

"This scarf is soaked with blood. Do you feel all right?"

Fatigue dragged at me. "Yeah. We need to call the Order of the Magica. Tell them something is up with the portal."

"I will."

I swayed on the table. "I don't feel so—"

The edges of my vision blackened. I reached for Aidan, but blackness took me.

I woke, my head foggy. I was no less exhausted. Darkness cast the room in shadows. I blinked, trying to make out the blurred shapes. Aidan slouched in a big chair near the bed, his chest rising and falling slowly. A sliver of light shined from the crack in a door, highlighting his face.

Asleep.

The bed felt like heaven, the sheets like they were a million thread-count.

"Hey." My voice scratched my throat.

Aidan jerked awake, his eyes meeting mine. "Hey, how you feeling?"

"Like shit."

"No surprise. You lost a lot of blood, as it turns out. That knife wound nicked some big veins."

Just my luck. "How's Dr. Garriso? Nix and Del?"

"He's fine. Sleeping in a room down the hall. Nix and Del also."

"Are we at your place?" I knew he had a big house in Enchanter's Bluff, the richest neighborhood in town, but I'd never been there.

"Yeah. It's close to the hospital. And the security is excellent."

I thought of the demons who'd showed up at P & P yesterday looking for FireSouls, and was glad to be here. And not just for the great sheets.

"Does the Order of the Magica know what's wrong with the portal?" I asked.

"No. But they're trying to work on it."

Shit. For being the most powerful magical organization in the world, they didn't seem to know their ass from their elbows. Or this wasn't a priority for them.

"We'll figure it out tomorrow," Aidan said. "It's still the middle of the night. And you're recovering."

My body felt like it weighed a million pounds, so he was probably right. I wasn't about to charge at the portal in this shape.

"Why are you in that chair?" I asked. "This is a big bed."

"Didn't want to disturb you. And I'm not in the habit of getting into bed with women unless I've asked them first."

I grinned. But he was right. We'd only slept in the same bed once, and I'd been healing that time too. Every time I got near a bed with Aidan, I was too wounded to do anything about it besides sleep.

I really needed a lifestyle change.

"Come on, sleep here with me," I said, exhaustion slowing my voice. "I need at least another few hours. And that chair can't be comfortable."

"It's not." He rose and walked around the bed, then climbed in behind me.

I scooted over to climb into his arms and kiss him, but it felt like moving through sand. So I settled for just cuddling up against him. He wrapped a big arm around me and tugged me closer. Comfort—belonging—welled within me.

Aidan leaned down and kissed the top of my head. "You doing okay otherwise?"

"Yeah." The memory of the other FireSoul in the desert drifted behind my eyelids. I shivered. "There was another FireSoul at the waypoint. When I was separated from you and my *deirfiúr*. I had to kill him to escape. I didn't want to steal his power, but it was so valuable. Illusion. It would have been stupid to leave it behind to prove something to myself. So I stole it, but this time it wasn't so bad. I think I had control."

"That's all that matters. As long as you made the decision consciously, you're improving."

I smiled. "I hope so."

But as sleep tugged at me, I remembered the joy that had surged when I'd taken the Illusionist's power. The smile faded from my face.

My heart pounded against my ribs as we crept down the darkened hallway. The stone floor was cold under my bare feet, and the chill air crept through my thin dress, though no worse than I was used to.

The dark cell we'd lived in for months—years?—had been colder than this. Darker than this.

"Hurry," the girl behind me whispered.

"Shh," hissed the girl behind her.

My two friends, though I didn't know their names, had escaped with me from our cell just minutes ago. I'd killed the guard who'd come to take one of us. Girls they took came back different. Or they didn't come back at all.

I'd stolen his magic before I'd killed him, though I had no idea how. It thrummed in my veins, an electric sensation that I didn't understand.

I tried to keep my breathing quiet as we moved down the hall. When we'd been in our cell, we'd rarely seen guards, but they could patrol these halls. My friends and I were only fifteen—at least, that's what I thought—and all of us were weak from malnutrition. Though I'd fought off the one guard, I knew I couldn't do it again.

We had no idea where we were, or how we'd gotten here, only that we had to get out. That meant moving forward, though I was so tired I wanted to lie down on the cold, hard floor. I'd grown accustomed to sleeping upon it and could be dreaming in seconds.

But if I did that, I'd never wake up.

Heavy wooden doors ran the length of the hall to our left. We didn't dare open them, though I'd have bet anything they were locked. A dark wooden door marked the end of the hall.

I glanced back at my friends. Frightened blue and green eyes met mine, wide in pale faces. They both nodded. I turned back to the door and gripped the handle, praying.

It opened.

Probably because the cell doors were locked and the inhabitants kept starving. How would they ever escape?

But we had.

Almost.

We crept silently up the stairs, stiffening at every little noise. The hair on my arms stood on end, prickling uncomfortably. When we reached the top, I was vibrating with fear. Slowly I pushed the door open.

A dimly lit hallway stretched out on either side of us. Wood floors and pale silk wallpaper gleamed dully in the light of oil lamps. The luxury of the hall was so at odds with the dungeon below that it turned my stomach.

Whoever had imprisoned us liked the good life.

The smell of dark magic stuck in my nose, making me gag. It smelled like rot and decay. Tentatively, we stepped out into the hall. As soon as I crossed the threshold, my soul felt lightened. Buoyed. The magic that seethed in my veins became more comfortable. As if it fit me better. Or worked, somehow, whereas once it hadn't. Maybe the dungeons had suppressed our magic.

I looked at my friends, startled by how thin and drawn they looked. As if they'd lived underground for a year and were just now seeing the sun.

Which I supposed was almost true. And I probably looked the same.

I jerked my head left and right, silently asking which direction to go. They both shrugged. Frustration welled within me. We were so close. I just wanted to escape.

An invisible, almost intangible tug about my middle pulled me left, so I followed it. Our bare feet were silent on the smooth wood beneath. We came to an open door on our left and stopped, peering in. An expansive library spread out before us, thousands of books tucked neatly into dark wooden shelves. A fire crackled warmly, making me ache to feel its warmth.

I looked away, searching the room for a person. None. We crept past the door, repeating our inspection at the next two rooms, a sitting room and an office. We were nearly to the end of the hall when a noise sounded from the open door ahead.

I stiffened.

Someone was in the next room.

The girl behind me gripped the back of my thin dress, tugging me to stop. It was unnecessary. I halted, dead still and trembling. The same dark magic scent seeped from the room ahead, turning my stomach.

Slowly, silently, we crept forward.

"You've disappointed me, Villiers," a cold voice said from within the room.

"Master, I'm...I'm sorry. I didn't mean to." The voice trembled, weak with fear.

"You know I can't have that kind of poor performance within my ranks."

"I know. I know. I will do better."

"I am not so sure."

I shuddered at the tone, so cold and dark.

"Please, Master. Just one more chance."

"I think not, Villiers. I am no longer patient with you. You don't make proper use of your gifts. I thought I'd give you a chance to prove yourself. To use your gifts on my behalf. But I see I was wrong to do so. I could make much better use of them."

"No!" A scrambling noise sounded, as if the man were trying to run away.

A crash and a scream.

The hair on my arms stood up as dark magic welled, feeling like bee stings against my skin. It came from the man with the cold voice. It had to. And he was going to hurt the other man.

He needed help. I had no idea if we could provide it, or if I was even brave enough to try, but I crept forward, compelled. Slowly, I peered around the side of the door.

A tall figure, dressed all in black, clutched a smaller man by his shirt. My heart thundered and my skin turned ice-cold.

"No!" The smaller man cringed away.

My foot twitched, as if to step forward, but I caught sight of the smaller man's face then.

One of the guards.

Then the scarier man must be the one in charge. The Master. He gave the command to keep us locked up. He took the girls who disappeared.

My foot stilled. I watched, appalled, as the dark magic swelled in the air and gray flame licked over the skin of the Master. His face twisted in pain, then in joy, as the flame spread onto the smaller man, enveloping him.

"I am going to enjoy this," he said. His voice was cold and precise. So controlled that he bit off each syllable with a crunch.

The smaller man screamed, his eyes rolling back in his head. The flame enveloped them both.

I backed away, horrified, then glanced back at my friends.

"Run," I mouthed.

Now was the best time. The Master was distracted. He was the biggest threat.

On silent feet, we raced past the door. Fear banished my caution. We sprinted out of the hall and into a great foyer. The glass dome above gleamed with light. Great wooden doors on the other side of the foyer beckoned.

Freedom.

My feet pounded the marble floor as we ran from this nest of vipers, desperate to reach the outside. I grasped the brass handle and flung open the door, throwing myself out into the sunlight.

I stumbled in sand. Fell to my knees.

When I looked up, a great golden desert spread out before me. We'd never make it across that endless ocean of sand with nothing but what we had on our backs. And we couldn't go back into the mansion.

We were trapped.

CHAPTER SIX

I woke with a scream strangling in my throat, sweat dripping down my body. I thrashed in the covers, scrambling from the bed and thudding to the ground.

My breath heaved as my gaze darted around the room.

It was big. Filled with heavy wooden furniture and an oriental rug that looked expensive. Whimsical landscapes adorned warm brown walls. Sunlight gleamed through the windows.

Aidan's house. I was in Aidan's house.

I peeked over the edge of the bed, praying that Aidan wasn't still there.

It was empty save for rumpled sheets.

I collapsed back onto the floor, trying to catch my breath.

I was going nuts. Clearly going nuts.

Between my magic and the nightmares, I was losing it. I sat there for several moments, trying to still my heart. I scrubbed a hand over my face, trying to rub the sleep from my eyes.

Cowering here on the floor wasn't going to get anything useful done. Not to mention, it was embarrassing. And right now, there were a lot of useful things I needed to be doing. Checking on Dr. Garriso, finding out what was up with the museum, getting my act together in general.

I climbed to my feet, still woozy from adrenaline, and found the beautiful bathroom. White marble gleamed, a modern masterpiece that was entirely unlike the tiny bathroom in my own place. There were no toiletries on the counter save the soap and a package of unopened toothbrushes, so this was clearly not Aidan's bathroom.

Damn. I'd have liked to have seen what his looked like.

I showered quickly, grateful that the healers had managed to close the wound on my arm. When I made my way back into the bedroom, I found my duffle bag on the chair. I hadn't heard anyone come in, so it had to have already been there. One of my *deirfiúr* must have gone back to our places to get clothes.

I changed quickly into my usual jeans and black t-shirt, and pulled a brown leather jacket out of the bag. I had dozens, most stored in my trove because they were technically treasure as far as my FireSoul was concerned, but I'd pulled this one out and put it on my bed the other day. Del or Nix wouldn't enter my trove without me. I wouldn't have minded, but we'd somehow silently agreed that was poor etiquette.

Properly dressed, I made my way through the house, seeking the kitchen. Aidan's Enchanter's Bluff home was far different than his place in Ireland, which was more modern. This place was more traditional. Very nice, but not my style.

I kinda had a feeling it wasn't Aidan's style either. But I guessed if you owned more than one home, maybe it didn't matter if they were all your style.

I followed the smell of coffee toward the kitchen, heading down an expansive wooden staircase and through a foyer to the brightly lit space where Aidan was serving coffee to Del and Nix.

They all glanced up at me.

"Feeling better?" Nix asked.

"Yeah."

"Good. Because you passed right the hell out last night," Del said. "Why didn't you tell us you were losing so much blood?"

"Didn't realize." I sat at the counter bar next to them. Aidan pushed a cup of coffee toward me. I reached for the cream and sugar and started to mix.

My exhaustion might have had something to do with stealing the other FireSoul's power, but I preferred not to think of that.

"How's Dr. Garriso doing?" I asked.

"Awake," Aidan said. "Still exhausted. But he said there are things he needs to tell us. We can go up in a moment."

"Good. We probably need to get a move on this quick," I said. "That portal changed a lot while we were inside it."

"And it's changed more," Aidan said. "The guard I bribed before has been calling me with updates. The portal has expanded. More of the museum is frozen."

Shit. "Any more people get stuck?"

"No. They've evacuated."

The situation was bad enough to abandon ship? Double shit.

Aidan turned and opened the oven to remove a foil-covered plate which he then put in front of me. He pulled off the foil to reveal bacon and eggs, still warm.

"Eat that. I'm going to go check on Dr. Garriso. We can talk to him when you're done."

I had a piece of bacon already in my mouth, my eyes nearly rolled back in my head at the taste of the fatty goodness. "Thanks."

He left the room, so freaking handsome and competent and good that it was like he was my own Captain America.

"Is he for real?" Del asked. She waved her hand around the kitchen. "Like, this rich and nice and cool and makes good breakfasts and everything?"

I swallowed the bacon. "Yeah, I think so. He said he's not great at cooking other meals, but apparently he can do breakfast."

Nix swiped a hand over her brow. "Whew. Glad he's not perfect."

"Whatever. He's a freaking unicorn and you know it," Del said.

"Yeah." I shoveled the eggs into my mouth. When I'd polished off most of the plate, I met Nix's and Del's gazes.

"You sleep okay?" Nix asked. "You still look pretty beat."

"Jeez, thanks." I scowled, then pointed at my eyes. "I happen to like storing my luggage beneath my eyes, actually."

Nix laughed.

"But you're right," I said, my light mood fading. "I didn't sleep great. I had another nightmare."

Interest flickered in their eyes. My nightmares had started about a month ago, ever since the Monster had reappeared in our lives. They were our only source of information about our past since our own memories were blacked out.

"Yeah?" Del said.

"Yeah. The Monster is a FireSoul."

Nix's coffee cup clunked to the counter. "For real?"

"Then why is he enslaving them?" Del asked.

"Doesn't want to do the dirty work, I guess." Though he had no problem doing the dirty work of stealing other people's powers. He'd been so like me when he'd done it, too. Such joy on his face. He'd wanted that power so badly. Again like me. But he'd been cold and controlled about it. Like I wanted to become.

My throat started to close up, my skin prickling, but I forced the feeling back.

Being cold and controlled about it was good. That was what I had to become. Aidan was right. I could fight this. I didn't have to become addicted to the power. It was my choice.

"So what happened in the dream?" Del asked.

90

I told them about how we'd escaped, about how the Monster had stolen the guard's power. My voice broke on the last part, about how he'd liked it so much.

Nix rubbed my shoulder. "What's wrong, hon? You've been so weird the last week."

I sucked in a ragged breath. How could I tell them? They didn't have anything like this problem. They didn't embrace their FireSoul selves at all. I felt more like the Monster than like them.

"Come on, 'fess up," Del said.

I met their gazes. Something loosened inside of me. They were my *deirfiúr*. They'd have my back. They'd *always* have my back.

"I'm afraid I'm changing," I said. I told them about the power, my need to steal it. About how I was getting better and gaining more control. Telling them about the Illusionist who'd been at the waypoint was harder, but I managed.

"But I still liked taking power," I said. "Stealing the Illusionist's power felt so good. That's sick."

"Duh, it felt good," Del said. "You beat the bad guy. He was going to leave Dr. Garriso to die in the desert and drag you off to make you a slave to the Monster. It's going to feel good when you beat someone like that."

"Yeah," Nix said. "You're not freaking Superman, all noble and shit. Able to take down the bad guys and not feel any dirty human emotions like victory."

"Hmmm." I guess they had a point, though I still felt off about it all. "I definitely am no Superman."

"Totally not," Del said. "You're plenty noble in your own way, but you're also really freaking human. You're just going to have to get over that."

Del knew I liked to hear it straight, and I was grateful.

"Thanks, guys." I reached out and squeezed both their hands. "I guess I'm just going kinda crazy with all these changes. After not using magic for so long and now having so much of it…"

"Not to mention the Monster coming for us. That'll make anyone nuts," Nix said.

"Yeah," I said. "Between him and those demons coming to P & P, it's like a noose is tightening around our necks. No matter where we turn, there are threats. And they're all connected—they have to be. But I have no idea how."

"I don't know either," Del said. "But we can start by figuring out what's going on at the museum. Let's go talk to Dr. Garriso."

"Hang on," I said. "There was one last thing about the dream. When we ran out of the house, it was into a desert. Rolling sand hills and everything."

"Like the waypoint," Nix said.

"Exactly," I said. "No one builds a mansion in the Sahara. I don't even think it's possible. Which leaves the waypoint. I can't say for certain that's where it was, but the similarity is too much to ignore."

"We were just at the Monster's headquarters. Is that what you're saying?" Del's voice quavered.

"Or at least nearby, in the world where he lives." He was the only person I couldn't find with my dragon sense. I'd seen him a week ago, but when he'd disappeared, I'd lost any connection to him. Like he'd left Earth entirely, which hadn't made sense at the time.

"I'd never thought of him being at a waypoint," I said. "But that's mostly because I didn't realize they existed."

"Don't feel bad. I thought they were a myth," Del said. "Even though I'd read about them."

"Well, now we know. So let's go find out more," I said.

It didn't take long to find Dr. Garriso, ensconced in a kingly bed on the second floor. He looked frail but chipper, like the experience couldn't keep his spirit down even if he might be under the weather for a while because of it.

Aidan sat beside the bed in a big chair. The windows behind him revealed an ocean view. The sea was iron gray today.

I glanced back at Dr. Garriso and asked, "How are you feeling?"

"Better." Dr. Garriso's voice was scratchy. "Thank you for rescuing me."

"Couldn't just leave you there, could I?" I sat at the foot of the bed. Nix and Del crowded beside me.

He smiled. "I did learn some rather, ah, interesting things while I was there."

"That's what Aidan said."

"The demons were never at the museum to steal something. They were at the museum to steal the museum."

"The museum?"

"Yes. The portal is a Massiva Domina portal. An old kind of magic. It will absorb the entire museum and transport it to the waypoint."

My breath whooshed out of me. "What?"

"The *entire* museum?" Nix said. "They're stealing the *entire* museum?"

"That's insane," Del said.

"But true," Dr. Garriso said. "I heard someone while I was at the waypoint. I don't know who. The walls between worlds are thin there. I do not think they realize that I heard them. Or even knew I was there."

"You didn't see who it was?"

"No," Dr. Garriso said. "Though his magic felt dark."

"That's the truth," Del said.

I'd bet money it was the Monster.

"The waypoint is many places at once," Dr. Garriso said. "Whoever wants the museum is using the waypoint as their base."

"They're not just collecting buildings, right?" I asked. "They want something that's in the museum."

"I don't know," Dr. Garriso said. "But I agree, it's safe to assume they are after an artifact. Since they couldn't remove it from the museum, they are taking the museum."

Ballsy.

"Could they be after the chalice?" I asked. My stomach dropped. "Shit. We left it at the museum. I was in such a panic over you—and I never imagined they could steal the whole museum—that I left it in your office."

"There are many valuable and dangerous artifacts at the museum," Dr. Garriso said. "Though they may be after the chalice. It's safe there as long as you stop the portal before it takes the museum.

"What is the chalice?" I asked.

"It has the power of Immortality. True immortality. No trauma or time could kill the person who drinks from the cup. But only the greatest evil can drink."

I swallowed hard. We'd never be able to get rid of him if he drank from the cup. "True immortality? That's a myth."

Dr. Garriso's expression became grave. "Not anymore."

CHAPTER SEVEN

"Ready?" Aidan asked.

"As I'll ever be." We stood at the edge of the library where we'd parked the car before. Mid-morning sun blazed down, too warm for my leather jacket. Thirty minutes ago, we'd left Dr. Garriso with Nix and Del and come to the museum.

Aidan glanced at his watch. "They should be there now."

I nodded. He'd made arrangements to meet with the Order of the Magica to discuss the portal and what we'd learned. Since I didn't want to be anywhere near them, I would sneak into Dr. Garriso's office to retrieve the chalice.

"All right. I'll meet you back here when you're done." I tucked the silver charm that hung around his neck beneath his shirt. "Remember to touch the charm to turn it on."

"I will."

"Good." Just because I wasn't meeting with the Magica didn't mean I didn't want to hear what was going on. I'd made Aidan take Del's comms charm. If he turned it on, I should be able to eavesdrop on the conversation.

He cupped the back of my neck, pulling me forward for a quick kiss. His lips were firm and warm beneath mine. An annoyed sound escaped me when he pulled away.

"Later," he said.

"Later. Once we're done saving the world and all."

He grinned, then turned and strode away.

I followed him around the edge of the building and stopped to watch him cross the street toward the front of the museum. My gaze skirted around the museum lawn. Empty.

Good. Safe to cross.

An idea popped into my head. It'd be even safer if I were invisible. And I might actually have the power to make that happen now.

But was I even capable of using the Illusionist's magic for that?

I glanced around again to make sure no one was near enough to sense my signature and called upon the Illusionist's magic. Unlike the lightning, which felt so obvious with its crackle and burn, this magic felt strange. Almost weightless.

I let it flow through me, making my limbs feel light, and envisioned myself disappearing. At first, nothing happened. But after a moment, my fingertips began to turn transparent.

Whoa.

Stealing this magic had been a damned good idea.

The sharp edge of guilt cut into me at the thought, but I shoved it away. As long as I wasn't driven nuts with power and didn't take from innocents, I was okay. I wouldn't end up like the Monster.

I focused on the magic and my desire to be invisible. To present the illusion that I didn't exist is how I thought of it.

Within a few seconds, I couldn't see my arms at all. I leaned down to check my appearance in the car's side mirror. My face didn't appear. Just the old library behind me.

Eerie.

I walked quickly across the street toward the museum's back parking lot. Magic prickled in the air. My skin tingled and my stomach turned. The portal was growing. I could feel it.

A squirrel ran right in front of me, glancing up confusedly.

So, either my head was now floating in the air or the squirrel could smell me but not see me.

I was gonna go with smell.

When I neared the museum, the bricks glowed slightly lavender. My stomach dropped. I hurried toward Dr. Garriso's window, weaving through the cars in the lot.

A flash of my hand caught my vision.

Shit.

I'd let my illusion waver and my body was becoming visible. This magic was still so new I had to really focus to keep it going. I tried my best to turn my mind toward the illusion, but the museum was damned hard to ignore. It was definitely turning purple.

By the time I made it to Dr. Garriso's window, I was invisible again. I peered in.

Holy magic.

Everything inside wavered, glowing with eerie purpleness. I reached out to touch the window, my fingers stopping at the glass.

Then the tips pushed through. A shudder ran over me.

The portal was modifying the glass, turning it from solid into the same soupy liquid feeling that had been in the artifact room when we'd escaped the waypoint.

My insides turned liquid with fear.

The whole museum was a portal now.

"Thank you for coming."

A voice radiated from my comms charm. I jumped back, a scream trapped in my throat.

Damn.

I panted. I'd been so distracted by the museum, I'd forgotten about Aidan meeting with the Order of the Magica. He must have turned the comms charm on.

"Absolutely," Aidan said. "I need to share what we discovered in the portal. And help any way I can with fixing it."

I listened with half an ear as Aidan described why he'd gone into the portal in the first place—to save his friend Dr. Garriso. The Order didn't like that he'd gone without informing them, but they sounded so freaked out about the museum that they didn't give him much hell over it.

And Aidan was a famous billionaire. Those types did pretty much whatever they wanted and got away with it, partially because the Order was so willing to cut him some slack. The system was rigged in his favor, but in this case, since I was on his side, it was in my favor too.

I glanced back at Dr. Garriso's window and the purple glow within. There was no way I'd be getting into Dr. Garriso's office to retrieve the chalice—not if I wanted to get out again—so I crept around the side of the museum to spy on Aidan and the Order investigators.

Tall bushes surrounded the museum and I crept behind them, keeping myself between the foliage and the brick. I let the invisibility illusion fade so that the Order couldn't sense my signature when I was close.

When I neared the corner of the building, I turned my comms charm off and relied on my regular hearing, calling upon a bit of my Shifter senses to help. I was practiced enough with it by now that I hoped my signature would be minimal. It seemed safer than leaving my comms charm on. What if the Magica heard it? Aidan's voice being echoed back would be super suspicious.

I peered through the bushes. Aidan stood in front of the museum's main steps with three figures. The investigators we'd seen the other day, minus the one who'd been frozen by the portal.

"So whoever is behind this is attempting to steal the museum," Aidan said.

"But you don't know what they want inside?" the female lead investigator asked.

"No." He didn't mention the chalice.

"It won't matter if he gets the museum," the male investigator said. "The whole town will be destroyed."

"Destroyed?" Aidan's voice was sharp.

"When the museum is sucked through the portal, nothing will replace it," the man said. "It will become a magical void. A vacuum that'll suck in the rest of the town."

I stifled a gasp.

"Massive casualties," the lead investigator said. "Unless Origin Enterprises can provide some kind of security for the town, we're going to have to evacuate."

They wanted Aidan's company to protect the town?

"We were hoping that your company could create some kind of barrier to keep the portal's magic from affecting the town," the male investigator said. "We understand that Origin Enterprises has developed enchantments for that kind of thing."

Aidan scrubbed a hand over his face, weariness evident in the gesture. "On a small scale, yes. We can protect a building from outside enchantments and spells, but not a whole town. At best, we could protect a few buildings in Magic's Bend. Given enough time, we could enchant them all, but that would take months. Maybe a year."

My heart thundered so loud I feared they would hear it.

"We don't have months," the female investigator said. "At the rate of expansion, we have days. The portal has almost encapsulated the entire museum. It'll begin to disappear soon."

"What if we try to strip the magic from the portal?" Aidan asked.

His Spell Stripper, I realized. But it was so small. No way it could do the job.

"There's only one person we know of who can do that, and we cannot find him," the lead investigator said.

"I wasn't thinking of a person," Aidan said. "I possess a Spell Stripper."

The investigator's eyes widened.

"Those are rare," the lead investigator said. "How did you come by one?"

"Heirloom," Aidan said. "I don't use it, of course, but it's been passed down in my family."

I squinted. He was lying, but I didn't blame him. However he'd come upon the Spell Stripper, no one would want the head of a security company to own one. They could break right in to whatever they'd protected. It was a nifty piece of magic, though. Anyone who could afford one would go for it.

"It's not large," Aidan said. "But if you have Amplifiers, it might work."

Not a bad idea. I'd never met an Amplifier before, but they were a type of Magica who were able to increase the magic they came into contact with. It was a handy skill.

The investigators looked at one another, then back at Aidan.

"We have two Amplifiers who work with the Order," the lead investigator said. "One on commission who lives in Magic's Bend, actually. We can have them here in a couple of hours. In the meantime, we'll issue the order to evacuate the city. Just to be safe."

"Good idea," Aidan said. "I have no idea if this will work."

I met Aidan back at the car.

"We need to go make sure Del and Nix evacuate. And Connor and Claire," I said. "And Dr. Garriso."

So many people I loved. And my trove. My heart constricted at the thought of my treasure. My friends would get out, but not my trove. If Magic's Bend were destroyed, it would be too. There was no time to evacuate the contents.

I grimaced, ashamed at the thought. Families would lose everything. Some people might not even get out soon enough. Now was not the time to be worried about my treasure.

Aidan drove like a madman, cutting through traffic. I called Nix on my comms charm, telling her to get Del and meet at P & P.

"I'll drop you off at P & P," Aidan said. "You can make sure Connor and Claire evacuate. I'll go get Dr. G."

"Connor and Claire can come pick him up," I said. "Then I'll meet you back at the museum. I can use my Mirror Mage powers to help with the amplification."

Aidan's knuckles whitened on the wheel, and I could tell he wanted to tell me to evacuate with the rest. But he also knew it wasn't my style, so he didn't bother.

"Good idea," Aidan said.

"I thought so."

Aidan pulled up to the sidewalk in front of P & P. I leaned over and kissed him hard, and then climbed out.

"As soon as this is all over, we're having that date," I said. I waved my finger in the air to indicate everything around me. "Because this is getting ridiculous."

"Agreed." He gave me a heated look. I shivered. "I'll meet you at the museum. Stay out of sight when you get there."

"I'll do my thing from behind some cover."

"Good. Be safe." He drove off.

I turned and entered P & P, just in time to see a blue light begin to glow in the middle of the room. The emergency announcement. Its glow turned the faces of the dozen patrons blue as they turned to it, their eyes wide with fear.

We hadn't had one of these in decades. Never in my lifetime. I'd only heard of them.

A voice boomed from the light, deep and authoritative. "This is a state of emergency. Evacuate Magic's Bend immediately. Threat of possible destruction of the town has been identified."

The voice continued to repeat the message. Patrons surged to their feet, grabbing bags and shoving chairs. Del and Nix were nowhere to be seen.

"Don't worry about your checks," Connor called from behind the counter. His face had paled, giving Snow White a run for her money. "Get out of here."

I hurried over to Connor, whose wide gaze met mine. "What's the deal?"

"There's a crazy portal at the museum. It's going to go nuts at some point and create a magical vacuum that will suck in the town. You've got to get out of here."

"Claire is on a job." His brows lowered over worried eyes.

"Call her. Have her meet you at Aidan's place in Enchanter's Bluff. I need you all to get Dr. Garriso. Del and Nix will meet you there, and Del will transport you out of town."

He nodded, reaching for his cell phone.

"I'm going to go find Nix and Del. They should be here by now." I ran from P & P, sprinting past Ancient Magic when I realized the shop was empty.

I disengaged the enchantments on the green door and took the stairs two at a time. I passed the second floor where Del lived, but by the time I reached the third floor, I realized I'd probably better check on them. They might be on their way, but they might also be distracted. I'd been so desperate to get to my trove that it hadn't crossed my mind.

I pounded on Nix's door. She didn't answer.

Shit. Where was she?

I pushed open the door. The small living room was empty. It was much better decorated than mine, though still tiny.

"Nix?" I called as I walked to her bedroom.

She stood in front of the open door to her trove, frozen.

Oh no.

Distracted.

I ran to her and grabbed her arm, tugging her backward. "Come on, Nix. We can't take it. We gotta go."

Her glazed eyes met mine. "Leave it all?"

"Yeah. We gotta." I thought of the locket in the back of my own trove. The only thing I had of my parents. At least, I thought it was from them. I had no memory of it or them, only that I'd been wearing the locket when I'd woken at fifteen with my past completely blacked out.

I couldn't leave it.

"Pick one thing, Nix. Whatever you can carry. I'll be right back."

She nodded, her eyes vacant. I hoped she'd be ready when I came back.

I sprinted back down the stairs to Del's door on the second floor. No answer. I pushed it open and went through to Del's bedroom. Like Nix, her trove door was open, but Del stood at the foot of the bed, shoving stuff into a big duffle bag.

She glanced up, her gaze wild. "I'm coming. I just had to get some things."

At least she was more conscious than Nix. "Good. Hurry. Nix is in a bad way. Meet me at her place."

"You going to your trove?"

"Yeah. Come get me if I'm not out in three."

Del glanced at her trove door. "Yeah. Yeah, I can."

"You gotta, Del. We've got to get Connor and Claire and Dr. Garriso out of Magic's Bend. You're the only one who can do it."

She nodded, some of the wildness leaving her gaze. "Yeah. I can do it. Can't get them too far because I'm still regenerating power from the portal, but I can at least get them a couple hundred miles away."

"Good. That'll do."

I left, racing up the stairs and through my apartment. My heart clenched. I'd miss this place if it got sucked away.

In my bedroom, I placed my hand on the wall where my trove was hidden and pushed my magic into the secret door, igniting the spell that would unlock it. The magic snapped, and I pressed the door open.

I flicked on the lights. Racks of gleaming weapons and supple leather jackets and boots filled the space. Contentment immediately flowed over me, filling me with warmth.

It reminded me of being with Aidan, and if that weren't screwed up, I didn't know what was. Human companionship and healthy relationships should probably be the number one source of comfort and joy in my life. Instead, it was my trove.

But maybe not for long, if the portal went out of control.

I forced myself to move quickly through my trove toward the back. When I reached the last alcove, I dropped to my knees and shoved aside an old pair of boots, then pressed my hand to the wall near the floor.

A small door swung open, revealing my little safe. The place where I kept my true treasures. It had once housed the Chalice of Youth and the Scroll of Truth, but now held only the small golden locket. Dr. Garriso had the chalice, and I'd given the scroll to Aidan for safekeeping.

I reached in and grabbed the locket, then shut the door and rose. As I walked back through my trove, I fixed the locket around my neck, wishing I could remember how I'd gotten it.

As I neared the exit, my steps lagged. My dragon sense ignited, trying to pull me back toward my treasures. I gritted my teeth and fought it, but it was like that part of my soul knew I was abandoning what we had worked so hard for.

Would my FireSoul rather stay and die than leave all this? Was it that powerful?

No.

I was in control. I'd been proving it these last few days, and I would keep doing so.

But I turned and took one last long look at the shelves full of my treasures, hoping I'd be back and that it would all still be here. Being a FireSoul might have come with a lot of power, but it came with even more baggage.

In this case, almost literal. I had to tear myself away, digging my fingernails into my palms to clear my head enough to find the strength to leave.

I didn't look back as I walked out the apartment door and took the stairs two at a time to Nix's place. When I entered, Del was dragging Nix out of the bedroom. Nix's glazed eyes met mine.

"Time to go," I said.

"But—"

I grabbed Nix's arm, cutting her off, and helped Del drag her out of the bedroom. By the time we made it to the bottom of the stairs, Nix's vision had cleared a bit.

"Thanks, guys," she said. "Don't know what came over me."

Del stayed behind and reignited the protection spells on the door while Nix and I headed to P & P.

"You're going to go to Aidan's and get Dr. Garriso with Connor and Claire," I said. "Then get out of town."

"What about you?" Nix asked.

"Going to help Aidan try to get rid of the portal. But I'll be right behind you."

"I want to stay and help."

I squeezed her hand.

"Me too." Del's voice came from behind. She'd run to catch up.

"Thanks, guys. But the only reason I can help is because I'm a Mirror Mage. There wouldn't be anything for you to do. And Del, you definitely have to get our friends out of town."

People would be fleeing by road, air, and magic. Magic was definitely the fastest.

"Yeah," Del said. "But I can come back."

"And I can just—" Nix halted and grabbed our arms, jerking us to a stop next to her.

"Look," she whispered, nodding her head into the window of P & P.

Another Tracker demon. The same kind who'd been hunting us before. Through his hair, I could just make out his sawed-off horns, and I'd bet anything that his eyes were that eerie silver.

"Oh, hell no." *Now?* "Doesn't he know we're evacuating?"

"Not if he just teleported here."

"Gotta love his timing."

This demon needed to be sent back to his hell, and fast. But the desire to confirm that he wasn't looking for us specifically tugged at me. If I was going to question him, I had to do it fast.

"I've got an idea." I sucked in a calming breath and called upon my new Illusion power. It was hard to get a grip on since I hadn't used it before, but I managed. Magic, fluid and ephemeral in this form, flowed through my veins. I imagined myself changing shape, growing horns and turning my eyes silver. My limbs didn't fill with warmth like they did when I actually shifted into animal form, but a sparkling sensation slid across my skin.

"Whoa." Del stepped back.

"How do I look?" I asked.

"Scary as fuck," Nix said. "Like a bigger version of that dude."

"Perfect. Follow me, but linger near the door like you're not with me."

They nodded.

I turned and strode toward the door, ducking as I entered. I probably didn't need to, but if I was bigger than the Tracker demon currently interrogating Connor, the illusion that covered me likely would have hit his head on the doorjamb. I caught sight of myself in the antique mirror behind the bar and almost winced.

I was one scary bastard, over seven and a half feet tall and built like a 'roided up wrestling star on Saturday morning TV. I twisted my features into a snarl.

"You!" I barked, pointing one massive finger at the other Tracker demon. "Why're you poaching on my turf?"

He spun, confusion on his beastly face. "Master's orders. Hunting FireSouls."

"You got a special assignment? 'Cause I do. One FireSoul in particular. You screw it up poking around because you're here on a general hunt and you'll fucking regret it." I prayed that's what they called them as I took a threatening step forward. I was half a foot taller than this guy and easily fifty pounds heavier.

"Hey, calm down. I'm just here on the seer's orders that there are FireSouls in this town. Not hunting anyone in particular. So if you are, I'll back off, let you have the bounty." He raised his hand.

Bingo. Just what I'd wanted to hear.

Connor's startled gaze darted between me and the other demon. He was reaching under the counter, possibly for a potion bomb. I needed to end this before he chucked the thing at me.

I called upon my lightning, letting it crackle and fill me. When I'd created a big enough bolt, I let it fly at the demon. Thunder cracked as he dropped like a stone.

"Cass?" Connor asked, bewildered.

I dropped the illusion and grinned. "Yep."

"I thought that smelled like you. Badass power."

"Thanks. I got it from a real asshole." I walked over and kicked the demon. He didn't budge.

Del approached. "That was some quick thinking."

"Thanks. Most of the times I try to wound and then question, I just end up killing. This seemed better."

"Yeah," Nix said. "At least we know they aren't hunting us in particular."

"Just that they know some of our kind live nearby." I grimaced. "Which isn't good."

"Let's not worry about that now," Del said. "We need to get out of here."

"Agreed." I hugged her, then Nix. "I'll call you when we're done at the museum."

CHAPTER EIGHT

This time, I spied on Aidan and the Order from the parking lot across the street. I stood behind a tall pickup truck, with a view through the window to the museum. It wasn't perfect cover, but everyone would be staring at the glowing museum, so I'd probably be fine.

I'd used the comms charm to tell Aidan where I would be. When I arrived, he'd perked up and looked back, his gaze searching the lot. He'd been listening for me with his Shifter hearing, I realized.

I peaked my head out, and he caught sight of me. One corner of his mouth kicked up slightly, and he turned back to the others. I recognized the three investigators, as well as one of the other two figures. The Amplifiers. One was an unfamiliar man dressed in a blue suit, but the other was familiar.

Mordaca?

Her dark hair and gown—she was basically a twenty-first century Elvira—were distinct. Mordaca was a Blood Sorceress who had a shop called the Apothecary's Jungle in Darklane, the part of town where most Black Magic practitioners lived and worked. She wasn't outright on the wrong side of the law, but there was no question she dabbled in forbidden magic. I'd hired her and her sister a month ago to help me find the Scroll of Truth, but hadn't seen her since. She must have been the local Amplifier the investigators had spoken about.

When she turned, I flinched. Could she see me? She didn't have any Shifter blood as far as I knew, so her hearing should be normal. How had she known to look back here?

"Why are you lurking?" A soft voice came from behind me.

My heart leapt as I spun, calling upon my lightning instinctively. It crackled under my skin.

"Don't shoot." A pale woman smiled eerily at me and raised her hands slowly. She wore a killer white pantsuit—that shouldn't look good on anyone but looked amazing on her—and her golden hair gleamed under the noon sun. Her magic sounded like chirping birds and felt like a light breeze, but she wasn't all goodness and light.

"Aerdeca," I said. Mordaca's sister. "What are you doing here?"

"Same as you. Keeping an eye on my loved one."

"Why is Mordaca here?"

"She's an Amplifier. The Order hired her to assist."

As I'd thought.

Aerdeca scowled. "But you're a Mirror Mage. You could be up there helping."

"I am. From here."

"Don't want to run into the Order?" She arched a perfect brow.

"No. Do you? You'd be better able to keep an eye on Mordaca if you were nearby."

"Fair enough. We'll lurk here together."

I turned back to the group and watched them talk. "I didn't know Mordaca was an Amplifier."

"She has many talents. But your magic feels a bit different than it did a month ago. I bet it's a *fascinating* story."

"No talking. Let's just watch."

Aerdeca shrugged.

"And give me space."

She moved back a few steps.

I turned my attention to the group in front of the museum. They were spreading out, Mordaca and the other Amplifier standing on either side of Aidan. They approached the museum and stopped about ten feet from it.

Aidan reached out, his hand slowly swiping through space. Testing the soupy portal air, I assumed. He then held the Spell Stripper out.

Magic swelled in the air as he activated it. The scent of the forest and the sound of crashing waves hit me. Then the Amplifiers's magic. The taste of whiskey came from Mordaca. The other Amplifier's power felt like a cold shower.

I shivered, then closed my eyes and tried to pick up the feel of the exact magic they were using. My chest thrummed with energy as I grasped the signature of the amplification and mirrored it. Like the power over illusion, this was harder than my usual magic. Probably because there wasn't something physical and easy to create, like fire.

My muscles vibrated with strain as I attempted to assist, but I'd had no training in this. It was like trying to grab on to eels. I visualized the amplification magic as green smoke that I pushed toward Aidan, trying to make it increase the Spell Stripper's magic.

"It's working," Aerdeca whispered. "Keep going."

Sweat dripped down my temples and my breath became short as I spurred my magic on, pushing it toward Aidan and the Spell Stripper. The museum wavered, the purple glow pulsing. The air began to thrum, as if the portal were fighting to hang on.

My legs weakened and I leaned against the truck. A hum sounded in my ears, either the portal's magic or my own exhaustion. I pushed past it, focusing on the whiskey taste and cold shower feel of the Amplifiers's magic.

"Whoa," Aerdeca whispered. "Keep going. The purple is almost gone."

She was right. I could feel the magic fading. The bricks of the museum were almost beige again. The air went deathly quiet as the portal finally faded. My heaving breath was the only thing in my head. I lowered my arms.

Aidan and the Amplifiers did the same.

The lightness of joy welled in my chest. We'd succeeded.

A thunderous boom cracked through the air, followed by a flash of purple. An enormous gust of power bowled me over.

Pain exploded in my entire body, tearing my muscles apart.

Then everything went black.

Golden light flared behind my eyelids.

The desert. Blazing hot light pounded down, but there was no sun. Magic vibrated in the air. The Monster, and something else.

I cringed, my stomach twisting with fear. I was back at the waypoint. The purple explosion of the portal flashed in my mind.

Had I been sucked in? Or was this a vision? It certainly wasn't like my dreams of my childhood.

I blinked and tried to push myself up, but I couldn't move. The hot sand sucked me down. My heart pounded. My panic tasted metallic. Was I paralyzed? I thrashed my head, trying to see if anything was coming for me. Trying to find an escape.

A flash of green caught my eye. I stared, squinting. An oasis. With a glittering blue pool in the middle. There was a hint of purple light in the middle of the water, and magic surged from it, rolling over me.

The pool was the source of the other magical signature—the one that wasn't the Monster—but it was strange.

I tried to focus on it, squinting to make out the purple light, but the glittering blue water kept distracting me. My brain felt so fuzzy that it was hard to concentrate.

It hit me a second later.

A Pool of Enchantment.

Of course. That was why we—

"Wake up!" A shriek tugged me from the desert.

I bolted upright, throwing off the hand that shook my shoulder.

"What? Where am I?"

"The museum, idiot! Now come help!" Aerdeca yelled. Her blue eyes were wild. Her power surged, egged on by her panic. She surged to her feet and darted off through the cars.

I scrambled up, panting. I wasn't paralyzed. I hadn't actually gone to the waypoint.

But the museum had.

"Oh shit," I breathed.

The east wing of the museum was gone. Or at least, mostly gone. I could catch the barest glimmer of the brick and windows, like a shadow. The rest of the building glowed a violent purple.

The portal had expanded. Big time.

Not only had we failed to get rid of it, we'd made it worse.

My gaze darted over the front lawn. Though it was a windless day, leaves skittered across the grass, drawn to the portal. A huge oak creaked as it bent toward the museum. Figures were scattered on the ground, frozen. The purple glow of the portal extended out over the grass like a dome.

Aidan!

I sprinted through the cars toward his prone figure. He was half in/half out of the portal's glow. Aerdeca was trying to push her way through the purple to reach Mordaca, whose body was fully encased in the expanded portal, her skin and clothes glowing eerily purple.

"Aidan!" I fell to my knees beside him. His eyes were closed, but his chest moved. "Wake up!"

I tugged at his shoulders, trying to drag him out of the portal, but he was too heavy. The portal must be pulling on him, because normally I'd at least be able to awkwardly tug his two-hundred-plus pounds.

I smacked him right across the cheek. "Wake up!"

He jerked, his eyes widening.

"What the hell?" He bolted upright and stared at his legs, encapsulated in the purple glow.

He tugged, then grunted. "Shit."

"You can't get out?"

Aerdeca's curses and magic flared from nearby as she tried to reach her sister. The other investigators and Amplifiers were all frozen solid within the portal.

"No." Aidan heaved himself along the ground, but he barely budged. "Move back."

His tone was so authoritative that I scrambled back without question.

Silver gray light swirled around him, and the evergreen scent of his magic swelled. He disappeared in the light, and an enormous golden blur burst forth, launching itself into the sky.

I tilted my head back. An enormous griffin soared above, its golden coat and powerful wings glinting in the sunlight. A grin spread across my face, and I jumped to my feet.

The griffin spun on the breeze and descended, landing with a thud that shook the ground.

"Not bad," I said, meeting its dark gaze. I couldn't help the shiver that raced across my shoulders at the sight of the beak that looked like it could crush cows. I knew he wouldn't hurt me, but he was still damned scary in this form.

Silver gray light flashed, and Aidan stood before me again, dressed in his same clothes, a talent I still admired. When I shifted, I ended up mostly naked on the return change. I'd managed to keep a single boot, my granny panties—it'd been laundry day—and my t-shirt last time, so I still needed more practice, but at least I was improving.

Aidan shook his head as if to clear it.

Aerdeca ran up, her gaze wild. Her immaculate suit was now streaked with grass stains from where she'd tried to crawl into the portal to reach her sister.

"How'd you get out?" she demanded.

"My griffin's strength. And because I was only half-captured." He glanced at Mordaca. "I can't help her. Not in the same way."

"Damn it!" Aerdeca hissed. "What is this? How do I get through it?"

"You can't," I said. "The portal is blocked from entry."

"It appears to be expanding just fine." Her tone was bitter.

My vision.

"I think there's a Pool of Enchantment fueling the portal charm," I said. "When I was knocked out, I had a vision. I think."

"You're not a seer," Aerdeca said.

"I know. But the portal is weird. And I've been through it before." In both the recent and distant past. "Maybe that helped. The portal leads to a waypoint. When you're there, you see all different worlds at once. I got a glimpse inside when it expanded."

"Or it's a fantasy you made up while passed out," she said.

"Or that." It was totally possible. "I may have invented all of this and not even realized it. But it's all I've got."

"What you're saying makes sense, though," Aidan said. "We put a lot of power into stripping the portal's magic. We almost succeeded, but it rebounded. It would need a lot of power to do that."

"Then we can't destroy the portal," I said.

"Not unless we go in. And we have some way of disenchanting the pool. We have to unhook the battery that's fueling the portal spell."

"So if we take the Spell Stripper into the portal, we can use it against the pond," I said.

"It's not nearly powerful enough. And it's there." Aidan pointed to the lawn. The Spell Stripper lay ten yards away, fully within the portal. No way to get to it, and apparently it didn't matter.

"Shit." I turned to Aerdeca. She was from Darklane and would have contacts even the Order of the Magica didn't. "Is there anyone in Darklane who might have a more powerful one?"

"I don't think so. They're too rare. And I'm not even sure a Spell Stripper would be strong enough. You need a Nullifier."

"Nullifier?"

"Someone with the power to undo magic."

I'd heard of Nullifiers before, but they were even rarer than FireSouls. "I have no idea where to find one."

"I might," Aerdeca said.

"How? Even the Order of the Magica couldn't find a Nullifier. They'd have used one if they could."

"The Order doesn't mix with Darklane. They don't know the things we do. Had Mordaca and I realized the power of the portal, we'd have suggested it. But they never asked. They think they side with righteousness, but their stubbornness just keeps them in the dark."

True. But wasn't that often the case?

"Go see Aethelred the Shade in Darklane. He's three doors down from the Apothecary's Jungle. In the blue building. Tell him I sent you. He may be able to point you in the right direction."

"Do you know anything about the Nullifier?" If I could learn just a little about him, it might be enough for my dragon sense to catch on. I could cut out Aethelred and find the Nullifier myself.

"I don't. Just that Aethelred once knew one. Or so he said. Over a glass of rum. So it might all be false."

Of course. "So basically everything we are going on might be false."

"But its all we have," Aidan said. "And all the representatives of the Order of the Magica are currently frozen in the portal, so it's just us now."

I liked Aidan's practicality. "What will you do?" I asked Aerdeca.

"Stay with Mordaca and try to get her out somehow."

I glanced at Mordaca's frozen form. *Good luck.* Hopefully she wasn't conscious.

"How long do you think we have?" I asked Aidan.

"No telling. But we should go now."

I looked at Aerdeca. "Call the Order of the Magica. Tell them what happened and what Aidan is going to try to do. See if they can help. But don't tell them I'm with him."

Part of me wanted them to know so I'd get the credit, just in case they figured out what I was and wanted to toss me in the Prison for Magical Miscreants. A history of saving Magic's Bend could only work in my favor. But a bigger part of me didn't want to appear on the Order's radar. If we actually succeeded in saving Magic's Bend, maybe I'd step forward. Get on their good side.

She nodded. "Fine. Give me your phone. I'll put my number in it. Call me when you know something."

I handed my phone over and waited, then Aidan and I hurried to his car in the library parking lot. I'd have to leave my car Cecilia and hope she didn't get sucked in.

As we were crossing the street, I touched the comms charm at my neck. "Nix? You get out of Magic's Bend?"

"Yes. We're in Portland at a human hotel."

"How's Dr. Garriso?"

"Fine."

"Good. Tell Del to rest up. We might need her to transport us through the portal again." I climbed into the passenger seat of Aidan's SUV.

"Will do. Can we help in any way?"

"Yeah, but not yet. We're hunting down a solution. I'll keep you posted."

"Good luck."

I turned off the charm and faced Aidan. His gaze was intent on the road as he sped through the nearly empty streets of Magic's Bend, weaving around cars loaded down with the belongings of fleeing citizens.

The worry I'd felt when I'd seen him trapped by the portal surged, like it'd been waiting for the first quiet moment to strike. I clenched my fists and swallowed hard, totally unused to this depth of feeling for someone other than my *deirfiúr*.

Unable to help myself, I reached out and laid my hand on his thigh.

He glanced at me. "You okay?"

"Yeah, great," I said, trying to turn the moment more casual. "This was actually how I'd been hoping to spend today."

He grinned. "My life is definitely more exciting with you in it."

"In the way surviving a train crash is exciting."

He squeezed my hand and turned onto Darklane. Ramshackle buildings rose three stories tall on either side of the street, their grimy facades glowering at us. The architecture was old, primarily Victorian, with intricate details and mullioned windows. Hints of bright paint showed through the grime here and there, but it did nothing to cheer the place up. Even the sun seemed blocked out. Darklane was Oliver Twistian in a haunted sort of way.

"Busier here," I said. There were more people in the streets, some still packing, others just observing. "Don't they know they're risking their lives?"

"Probably. But they're stubborn and don't trust authority."

"Apparently."

We passed the Apothecary's Jungle, its once purple facade somehow distinct among the rest of the grimy buildings. The brass lion door-knocker watched us drive past.

"There." I pointed to a building that had probably once been blue. It was three doors down, though, so it should be the place.

Aidan pulled the car over and I hopped out, then raced up the narrow steps to the wooden door. I banged the falcon door-knocker, warily watching its eyes. Aidan joined me on the stoop.

"It can see us," I whispered.

"And hear you," said a voice from the other side of the door. "Who's there?"

"Cass Clereaux and Aidan Merrick. Aerdeca sent us. We need your help."

"Never heard of a Cass Clereaux," the crotchety old voice said. "But Aidan Merrick, I've heard of. Imagine he'd pay well for assistance."

I glanced up at Aidan.

"I would," Aidan said.

The door swung open. A wizened figure dressed in a blue velour tracksuit eyed Aidan. A white beard reached nearly to his belt, and his eyes sparked with intelligence. He looked like Gandalf on his way to a senior aerobics class.

The sharp gaze dropped to me, then widened. "You."

"Me?"

The man shook his head, then stepped back. "Come in."

We followed him into the dark little foyer.

"What about me?" I asked.

"Come, come." He shuffled into a dark living room. Shades were drawn, casting faint light on the books and trinkets that spilled from the shelves lining every wall. Dust motes danced in the light, and a fire burned in the small iron hearth.

"What about me?" I repeated.

He turned, his gaze falling to the locket about my neck.

"Now is not the time," he said.

Frustration beat its fists against my chest. "Do you know about me?"

"I'm not sure. But now is not the time. You are here for help, and it's not about you or your past." He sat in a ratty armchair and gestured to the couch.

I hadn't mentioned my past, but him mentioning it got me thinking. I lowered myself onto the dusty fabric. "What I'm here about may be linked to my past."

He squinted at my locket. "It may be, yes."

"Sir, do you mind if we inquire as to your powers?" Aidan asked.

Points for politeness with the old dude. I just wanted to shake him until info fell out.

"Seer," Aethelred said. "Among other things."

"Is that why you aren't leaving Darklane?" I asked. "Will we succeed in saving the museum?"

His eyes sparked. "I'm not a fortune teller!"

"Sorry."

"Good. But no, I do not know if you will succeed in saving the museum. Though I did know that I was supposed to wait here to assist whoever was trying. When we are done, I will depart." His gaze swept sadly over the room. "I do hope you succeed."

"So you know what we're looking for?" I asked.

"I do not. So you'd best tell me. And quickly."

"A Nullifier. We need his help to disenchant something."

"Hmm… When I was young, I had a friend who was a Nullifier. He has been in hiding for centuries."

For *centuries*?

"They are hunted, you know," Aethelred said. "For their immortality."

"Immortality?" I was hearing that word a lot lately.

"Their power nullifies all magic. Even death. Trauma can kill him, but not time. He has been afraid someone will try to steal his power and immortality by murdering him."

"Fair enough," I said. Apparently there were folks out there who had it worse than FireSouls.

"What do you need one for? Not to kill him for his immortality, I presume?" Aethelred asked.

"Of course not." Immortality would be *awful*.

His gaze hardened. "Convince me. I won't send an assassin after my friend."

"I do *not* want his power," I said. Living forever would suck. Who wanted to watch all their friends and family die? "We need his help with a Pool of Enchantment."

I explained the waypoint and my vision, finishing by saying, "At least, I think it was a vision. I don't even know if it's true or if we're on the right path."

Aethelred glanced at my locket, then lifted a hand as if to touch it. "May I?"

I nodded.

His fingertip touched the small golden charm, and he closed his eyes.

"Your vision is accurate. This links you to your past, and the waypoint is from your past. The locket helped you have your vision." He removed his hand.

"Huh." I wasn't sure if I was happy or scared. I knew more about my past, but I didn't like what I'd discovered.

"Eloquent."

"It's a gift," I said. "Is there anything else you can tell me?"

His gaze turned solemn. "You are at a crossroads that few must face. One direction will call strongly, but you must resist. For your own good, and that of others. Your fears about yourself are valid because you face great darkness. But there is more than enough light within you to vanquish the dark, if you embrace it."

I tried to keep my breathing steady as I listened. None of this surprised me, but that didn't mean I had to like it. Having someone else confirm my fears was bad enough. That he thought I could fall to the darkness...

That was terrifying. I believed I was making progress—that I was more like my *deirfiúr* than like the Monster. But hearing my fears spoken aloud, by a seer no less, made it hard to remember the strides I'd made.

Did Aethelred know what I was?

"Is that all?" I asked.

"For now. Save Magic's Bend and my home, then we will talk. One is more time sensitive than the other."

"Fair enough. How do we find the Nullifier?"

"Outside of the village of Gimmelwald in the Swiss Alps."

Of course he lived in the Alps. Probably at the top of the highest Alp.

"Do you have a transport charm we could purchase?" Aidan said. "Or more? We will need to get to Switzerland quickly."

"Yes. You'll need them." He got up and shuffled from the room.

I glanced at Aidan. "Do you think he really knows about my past?"

"He could. He is a seer."

It killed me not to demand answers now, but he was right. Hurry didn't begin to describe our situation.

Aethelred returned and handed three transportation charms to Aidan. "This is all I have."

"What do I owe you?"

"If you succeed in saving the museum, nothing other than replacing those charms. If you fail, buy me a new house when this one is sucked into the magical vacuum. But I like this one, so hurry. You have a few days, at most. Changes are occurring quickly now."

Aidan nodded sharply and I winced, the reality of what was at stake clear. Many people would lose their homes. If they didn't leave Magic's Bend, they'd die. The biggest magical city in America would be destroyed. The damage could be so great that humans might notice.

A cold sweat formed on my skin. I did not like this kind of pressure.

We rose to go. As we left the room, Aethelred spoke.

"Oh, and two things."

I turned.

"Most magic will not work around the Nullifier, as I'm sure you can imagine. Suppressing other's gifts is how he protects himself. So unless you want to end up on the side of a mountain, I suggest you use the transportation charm to go to Stechelberg, the town nearest his, then approach using traditional means."

"How will we find him if I can't use my Seeker sense?" In public, I pretended to be a Seeker to explain why I could find things. No one wanted to kill Seekers.

"Look for the fairytale in the forest. You will find him."

"The fairytale in the forest?"

"You'll figure it out." He pursed his lips, clearly willing to tell us no more.

"All right. And the other thing you mentioned?"

"Do not lose that locket."

CHAPTER NINE

"Oh, hell no," I muttered as I stared up at the mountains that soared above us.

We'd transported to Stechelberg a moment ago and now stood at the edge of town. Dawn sun illuminated the mountains around us, casting the harsh faces in a soft glow. The craggy stone peaks rose vertically into the air, straight out of the green meadows in the valley.

My chest felt achy and empty, no doubt the Nullifier blocking my magic. It was awful. Nauseating.

"How the hell are we supposed to get up there?" I asked. "I can't see a road."

"I can't use my magic," Aidan said. "He must be blocking it. Feels like hell."

"Yeah, it sucks." I pressed a hand over my heart and sucked in a shuddery breath, then pulled out my cellphone and searched Gimmelwald. Damned data charges were going to kill me, but at least it was a business expense. "Yeah, no road access, according to Google. But there is the Stechelberg-Murren-Schilthorn aerial tramway."

"A cable car?"

"It's our best bet if there's one leaving soon." Instinctually, I called upon my dragon sense and thought of the tram station. When the familiar tug pulled against my waist, I opened my eyes.

"My dragon sense works," I said, surprised. Despite the gross feeling of having my power suppressed, my FireSoul ability still worked.

"Why?"

"I don't know. I didn't expect it to, but I'm so used to using it that I tried it when I wanted to find the station."

"Good. Don't look a gift dragon in the mouth. Use it."

"Come on, this way," I said. "It's not even half a mile."

We hurried through the small village of Stechelberg, passing down what looked like the main street. The wooden buildings scattered on either side had flower boxes hanging off the windows. Purple and red blooms tumbled out. It was all so charming that my eyes almost crossed.

"I swear, Heidi is going to run out any minute," I said.

Aidan laughed.

The houses gave way to open meadow, but at the end of the road, I caught sight of the station. It looked like a big, modern airplane hangar with cables rising into the air and up the mountainside.

We bought tickets and were the first—and only— passengers on the early morning ride up the mountain. As the cable car swung over the vast open space and the mountains below, I sat on the bench and lowered my head between my knees.

"Oh, I'm not built for this." My stomach heaved.

"You've ridden on my back just fine." Aidan sat next to me and rubbed my shoulders.

I reached for his hand and squeezed. "That's different. This was built by humans."

"They're good at building things. Better than Magica, really."

"They built the Titanic."

"True. But I doubt this will hit an iceberg."

"Knock on your head. Don't jinx this."

I looked up to see Aidan grin and knock on his head. The view out the window was spectacular, the craggy mountains reaching up to a pure blue sky. The higher we rose, the bigger they seemed, as if ever-extending vistas were being revealed with every meter upward.

"Do you feel that?" I asked. The empty sickness I'd felt down in Stechelberg was worse here, as if the Nullifier's no-magic zone were stronger.

"Yeah." Aidan's voice was raspy.

For Magica, our power was like part of our soul. An organ, almost. When it was repressed or removed— which was rare—it felt like hell.

"Oh, that's awful," I breathed.

The cable car slowed as it approached the Gimmelwald station. Unlike the last station, the mechanical apparatus for controlling the cables was out in the open, crouched on top of the station building like a great iron dragon.

"Loving this," I muttered as my stomach turned. Losing most of my magic combined with motion sickness was not fun.

The second the car stopped, I hopped off and rushed down the stairs to solid ground. Aidan followed at a less freaked-out pace.

"Whew, that's better." Even ten seconds on real ground made my stomach feel less miserable.

Aidan rubbed my back. I couldn't help but smile.

We turned and looked toward the tiny town, which was just as quaint as Stechelberg, surrounded by the small valley and forest. We were stair-stepping our way up the Alps, from tiny valley to tiny valley. One day I wanted to come back here and climb those soaring granite peaks. I wasn't much of a hiker, but this was inspiring.

"So we need to look for the fairytale in the forest," Aidan repeated Aethelred's words.

"Then let's head for the forest." I cut across the narrow street and between two dark brown wooden buildings. The red and yellow flowers in the window boxes gave off a sweet smell. Soon, we were hiking across the meadow to the forest ahead.

"Thank magic Gimmelwald isn't at the top," I said. The bare granite peaks glowered down at us.

"I just hope we're headed toward his forest."

I nodded. There was another forest on the other side of town, but it was down the mountain a bit and harder to get to.

Ten minutes after entering the meadow, we reached the woods. Trees towered in front of us, casting shade and dappled sunlight on the forest floor.

"I see no fairytales," Aidan said.

I focused on what little I knew of the Nullifier and called on my dragon sense. The familiar tug pulled around my middle. "Ahead, then slightly left."

Twigs crunched under our shoes as we cut between the trees. Squirrels stopped to chitter down at us, scolding us over some forest infraction. The air was fresh and bright, filling my lungs and my head with joy and clarity.

It was magical in the forest.

I could stay here forever, just walking and wandering amongst the sunlight glittering on the ground, listening to the squirrels admonish us from above. Peacefulness descended over my mind, a blissful serenity that edged out any of my worries.

A low, lovely noise reached my ears.

Humming.

I glanced at Aidan, turning my head slowly so as to preserve the perfect calm, and saw that he was humming some kind of tune, his face relaxed and his gaze calm.

Good. He was enjoying himself too.

I drifted along as we walked, following the sounds and scents of the forest. When glittering lights danced ahead of us, like fireflies in the daytime, I smiled and turned toward them.

Aidan followed as well, his steps relaxed beside mine. We followed the dancing lights through the forest, drifting along and enjoying the moment.

Wouldn't the morning be lovelier with a coffee? There was the nicest little bakery in town with the most delightful view of the mountains. We should go there. Have a coffee and enjoy the view. Perhaps even a pastry.

At this moment, there was nothing I wanted more than a pastry. I turned to go to the village, not even bothering to tell Aidan my new plan. He would want to do the same thing, too, of course. It was the most natural thing in the world to go to the village right now, so he would have the same idea.

As I'd expected, Aidan turned and followed me. The dancing lights accompanied us. Our new friends.

Friends... Friends...

Why was that word pulling at my mind? And what was the annoying tug about my middle? I wanted to go have a coffee in the village, not think about friends.

But my friends needed me. For something, something. And the tug about my middle was so insistent.

A chattering squirrel caught my eye, dragging my gaze from the glittering lights.

Clarity pushed at the edges of my mind, trying to drag my thoughts in one direction.

Friends... Friends...

Panic clawed at my throat, disrupting the lovely calm. My friends needed me. I was here to help them. But they weren't here?

I stopped and shook my head, then fisted my hands in my scalp, hoping the pain would clear my mind.

It did, enough that I remembered we were here to seek someone. The Nullifier.

136

Find the fairytale in the forest.

These lights were straight out of a fairytale, luring the unwary traveler off their path.

"Aidan, snap out of it," I said. "Don't look at the lights."

He shook his head. "What?"

"Don't look at the lights."

His gray gaze met mine, foggy with confusion. I reached out and pinched his arm. He jerked, but his vision cleared.

"Damn it," he said. "Enchantments."

"Yeah. Smart ones. Enough to keep the villagers away from the Nullifier's house. They told me to go to a coffee shop that I didn't even know existed." I closed my eyes and focused on my dragon sense, picking up the trail again. "Come on, this way."

We set off through the forest again. I danced my gaze around the forest, never resting on any one thing too long.

"We should talk," I said. "Ty to keep ourselves from falling under the forest's spell again."

"Good idea. First topic. Aethelred said some interesting things about the crossroads you face."

"Wow, you really jump into it, don't you?"

"I like to cut to the chase."

"Okay. Then yeah, I've got some thoughts. He's obviously talking about my love of power."

Aidan nodded.

"And that scares me," I said. "It makes it real."

"But it also means it's not just you."

"No, you're right. He said that others have faced this as well. And that they've succumbed." I shivered at the memory of my nightmare. "I had a nightmare at your house. A memory. The Monster is a FireSoul. *That's* what Aethelred was warning me against. Don't become like him."

"And you aren't."

"I'm more like him than my *deirfiúr*. They've never been tempted by their FireSoul power."

"They haven't been forced to embrace it like you have. You're doing it to survive, Cass. To protect the ones you love."

I glanced at him and realized his gaze had been on me. Sincerity shone on his face. He really believed what he was saying. I reached out for his hand.

"I know we haven't had time for that date I promised you," I said.

"I wasn't exactly expecting something traditional," he said. "Don't get me wrong—I'd take it. Dinner that isn't pasties from P & P and a walk on the water sound killer, but your life doesn't exactly leave room for things like that."

"No. You're right." I focused on my dragon sense. We were still going the right way. "But I'm glad you're on this, uh, adventure with me. My *deirfiúr* have always had my back, but having you, too, is pretty great."

"Thanks."

"You sure you have time to be always helping me out? You've got a giant business to run, right?"

"I believe in delegating. And there's not really a more pressing concern than saving Magic's Bend. It tops my list right now."

I laughed, both amused and distressed. "Well, I'll definitely take your help when I can get it."

"Good. You have it whenever you need it. And also when you don't need it."

Whatever we had between us, we were making it kind of official, I realized. I wished we had more time to just *be*—to go on that date, to find time for more. But for now, I'd take what I could get, even if it was just quickly stolen moments while looking for the fairytale in the forest. Maybe this was our thing.

I still didn't know if I was supposed to call him my boyfriend, but the word didn't really suit Aidan.

"Do you hear that?" he asked.

I tensed, perking my ears. When I heard nothing but the rustle of leaves and the chittering of squirrels, I shook my head.

Then a rumble sounded beneath the ground, as if tree roots were grinding against dirt and rock. The glittering lights hovered just out of the corner of my eye, but I forced myself not to look. They were a threat, but there was something else far below.

We were getting closer to the Nullifier. The tug around my waist was getting stronger, as was the gross feeling of having my magic repressed.

Suddenly, the ground in front of us exploded, tree roots surging up and dirt flying into the air. I lunged back.

Figures scrambled up from the earth, their short, dwarfish bodies formed from twisted roots. Color glinted here and there. Gems stuck in the crevices between their gnarled roots. Five root-dwarves, with more climbing out of the scar in the earth.

I pulled my obsidian daggers free from my thigh holsters and tossed Aidan one.

"We come in friendship, Nullifier!" I called.

The dwarves did not answer, however.

Their dark jewel eyes glinted as they charged us, their footsteps shaking the earth beneath them. They seemed to gain strength and power with every step, drawing it from the earth.

Three collided with Aidan as the other two clashed with me. One went low for my legs, while the other threw a mean right hook. I got my blade up just in time to sever his root-arm, but crashed to the ground as the other plowed into me.

I kept my grip on my blade. Thank magic for obsidian, the sharpest stuff on earth. Because obsidian was volcanic glass, my daggers had been enchanted not to break. I thrust it out as the dwarf lunged for me, sinking my blade into his chest.

He didn't even flinch. Instead, he gripped his rough, root-formed hands around my neck and squeezed. Stars burst behind my eyes as I gasped. I slashed with my blade again, swiping him across the face.

Again, he didn't react other than to squeeze tighter.

Damn it.

I raised my legs, tucking them under his body, and kicked with everything I had, throwing him off of me. I gasped raggedly at fresh air. He was silent as he flew through the air and crashed to the ground, but he scrambled up immediately. The other dwarf was so close I could make out the glitter of jewels stuck between the roots that formed his body.

If I couldn't use my magic or my blades, I had no idea how to beat these guys. Aidan was holding his own, but he couldn't kill them without magic.

I reached up and touched the comms charm around my neck. "Nix? Del? I need help!"

"What do you need?" Nix's voice came through.

Gratitude welled through me that the Nullifier's power hadn't disabled my charm. Possibly because it wasn't a kind of magic that could be used to hurt him.

A dwarf threw himself at me, taking advantage of my distraction. I crashed to the ground. Pain exploded at my back, like my ribs crunching.

"Dwarfs made of roots in Switzerland." I gasped as I wrestled with the dwarf. "Any way... to beat them without magic?"

"Okay, okay, on it. Give me a sec."

Nix was my remote backup on tomb raiding jobs, helping me with riddles and other challenges. Because so much was based on folklore, it often wasn't hard to find the answers to things through research.

"'Kay, dwarves are big in Swiss folklore," Nix muttered, no doubt scrolling Google. It was a little embarrassing that I was a tomb raider who relied on Google, but it worked so I wasn't going to give it up.

141

"Hurry!" I kicked the dwarf off me. He sailed through the air, roots flailing, but the next plowed into me almost immediately.

I glanced over at Aidan to see that he'd tied up his three using roots he'd pulled from their bodies, but three more had clawed their way out of the ground and were headed toward him. My gaze caught on the sparkling gems gleaming from the crevices between their roots, my dragon covetousness pinging. I'd like to pull those sparkles right off them.

The dwarf on top of me landed a sharp blow to my cheek, sending light exploding behind my eyes. Agony radiated from my cheekbone.

That was what I got for getting distracted by the shinies.

"Now, Nix!"

"Getting nothing here. Lemme ask Dr. Garriso!"

I thrashed with the dwarf who had me pinned, managing to slash off both his arms with my dagger. He didn't even flinch, which I was sort of glad about because the dwarves were cute in a gross way. His arms would grow back, but I hoped it'd buy me half a minute.

I scrambled away from his flopping form, but the other dwarf grabbed my ankle. This was becoming an exhausting cycle of incapacitating one dwarf just to have the next recuperate and attack.

"Cass!" Nix's voice blared. "Grab the gem in their forehead. Pull it out!"

Gem in their forehead? I twisted beneath the dwarf who'd grabbed me. He clambered up my body, swinging for my head. I ducked, then peered at the tangled roots that made up his craggy face. Gems for eyes, but no gem in his forehead.

I bobbed my head, as much to avoid his blows as to get a different angle to better see through the roots of his face. A tiny flash of red caught my eye, beneath the first layer of snaking roots. It was deep, damn it.

I sucked in a breath and plunged my hand through the roots. My knuckles burned as the wood gouged at my skin. Barely, my fingertips brushed the smooth stone, and I pushed harder, wincing. I tightened my fist around the gem and pulled it free.

The dwarf collapsed.

"Aidan!" I called. "Pull the gem out of their heads!"

The other dwarf barreled into me before I could get up. We wrestled, his small form shockingly strong. Eventually, I threw him onto his back and thrust my fist into his forehead. My hand screamed with pain, but I plucked the gem free.

I rolled off the dwarf, panting, my aching hand gripped around the gem.

"You okay?" Nix's voice sounded from the charm around my neck.

"Yeah," I panted and tipped my head back to see Aidan pulling the gem from the last dwarf. It collapsed into a pile of roots before being absorbed by the ground.

"Can I keep the gems?" I asked Nix.

"Hang on, lemme check." Muffled talking sounded from the charm. "No, sorry. Bad luck. Toss them back."

"Damn." My dragon sense winced as I tossed the glittering stone to the ground. The sparkling blue was immediately absorbed by the dirt. I scrambled to my feet.

Aidan walked toward me.

"Good thinking," he said. "How'd you know?"

I pointed to the charm. "I didn't. Nix did."

"Dr. Garriso, actually," Nix said. "We should keep him on retainer for tricky things like this. Our own phone-a-friend."

I laughed. "See if you can work something out. We've got to get going now. Thanks, Nix."

"Sure thing. Be safe. Call if you need anything."

"Will do."

I touched the charm to turn it off and flinched at the pain in my hand.

Concern darkened Aidan's gaze. "You okay?"

"Yeah, a little scratch." I eyed his big hand. It was beat up, but he didn't seem to notice.

"Hardly." He reached for my hand and lifted it, his touch gentle. "Let me take care of this."

"I don't think your magic will work."

"Let me just try."

I held out my hand. Healing warmth flowed from his touch. My pain leached away.

"Why does it work?"

"Maybe it's not a kind of magic that can hurt the Nullifier. Like the magic that fuels your charm. It's got to be exhausting to continually repress the magic around you. He probably saves energy by repressing only the stuff that could be harmful to him."

"Yeah, I guess. That feels amazing, thanks."

"No problem."

I couldn't help but notice he'd healed me before himself.

"One hundred percent?" he asked.

I flexed my hand. "Yeah."

"Good." He lowered my hand and let go. "Which way now?"

I focused on my dragon sense, thinking of the Nullifier and my desire to find him. The tug pulled at my middle. "Left."

"Lead on."

We set off through the forest. I kept my gaze active, darting from tree to shrub to sky, never landing on something long enough to become enchanted.

"You aren't going to heal your hand?" I asked.

"It's a little thing. I'll save the power. With the Nullifier repressing most of my magic, I don't know how much I have to draw on."

Like most Magica, Aidan had to regenerate his healing power if he used too much. We Magica were just magical rechargeable batteries of varying strength, though I didn't know what our source of power was. No one did. We were all just born like this. There were myths about our origin, of course, but they were so old I'd never thought they were important.

"I think we're almost there," I said after a few minutes of walking. "Somewhere near—" Magic vibrated in the air, strong enough to steal my breath. "Do you feel that?"

"Yeah." Aidan's gaze shot alertly around the forest. "Something is coming."

A shriek tore through the quiet, followed by the beat of wings and a whoosh of air. Aidan plowed into me, throwing me to the ground. My breath exploded from my lungs, and I stared dazedly at the sky.

Flame and smoke swooped in the air above, right where my head had been, followed by water and stone. I squinted, my head spinning from my fall.

"Dragons," I whispered as my vision sharpened.

CHAPTER TEN

The dragons were small—no bigger than dogs—but they were dragons. They swooped in the air above, each made of a different element. The fire dragon dive-bombed us, its flickering red body hurtling through the air, its orange eyes riveted to my own.

"Go!" I yelled.

Aidain rolled off me, and I scrambled away, dirt flying beneath my clawing hands. The fire dragon plunged low, its flaming orange belly singeing the grass. Up close, I could tell that it wasn't a flesh-and-blood dragon, but rather a creature made entirely of flame.

And the flame was very real. The grass was black where the dragon had flown.

Something hard hit me from behind, and I flew forward, landing on my face. Burning pain fired through my nose. Smoky wind rushed by my head, blowing my hair up.

The smoke dragon had nailed me.

I scrambled to my feet and spun, finding Aidan in the path of the fire and stone dragons. He lunged to the side, but the stone dragon got him in the arm, a blow so powerful that Aidan grunted, the first sound of pain I'd ever heard him make. His arm hung at an odd angle, limp at his side.

A freezing, wet force slammed into my head from behind, soaking me in a deluge of ice water that made my brain ache like an ice cream headache on steroids. I fell to my knees, my stomach heaving from the pain. Icy water dripped down my back, and my hair plastered itself to my head.

"We come as friends!" I shouted, my own voice making my head throb. The words sounded stupid—*take me to your leader-esque*—but I couldn't think of anything else with my brain frozen.

Heat flared at my back. The fire dragon! I dodged just in time, throwing myself to the ground before it lit me up.

These little bastards were pissing me off!

I scrambled to my feet just as Aidan swung a tree branch with his good arm. It cracked against the stone dragon, who'd been headed straight for my skull, and the little monster hurtled in the other direction, head over tail. It caught the air under its wings again, flying high and uninjured.

"Ideas?" Aidan muttered, chucking his broken branch aside. He gripped his dislocated arm and shoved it back into its socket, grunting.

What a badass.

My head still ached, and I was soaked to the waist. I so did not have the energy or the patience for this.

I spun to face the smoke dragon that hurtled toward us. Its gray gaze met mine as it charged.

I held out my hand, something unfamiliar but natural urging me on, and commanded, "Halt!"

The wispy gray dragon pulled to stop in midair, confusion sparking in its silver eyes. Out of the corner of my vision, I caught sight of the fire dragon doing the same.

"They've all stopped," Aidan said.

"Yeah."

My dragon sense, which up to this moment I'd only used to find treasure, tugged in my chest. Like it recognized these little guys.

"I've got no idea why," I said, though I knew it had to have something to do with my FireSoul. I wanted to play with that info for a little while before sharing it. Even though Aidan was such a smart guy that he'd probably make the connection anyway.

"You didn't mirror my Elemental Mage powers?" Aidan asked.

"No." Though it might have worked, considering these tiny dragons were made of the elements.

I twisted my hand so I held it palm up and beckoned. "Come here."

The smoke dragon tilted its head, its gaze considering.

"I won't hurt you," I said. "Now, come here."

Its wings beat twice, sending it drifting on the wind, until it sat on my palm. It was about the size of a terrier, balancing easily on may hand. Warm tingles spread across my skin and up my arm.

Kin.

The feeling was so strong, so real, that I couldn't ignore it. Was this a real dragon and not just an apparition of magic? It was so tiny. And no one had seen a real dragon in centuries. I peered at the dragon, trying to find something—anything—that made sense about it.

"Are you an apparition?" I asked the dragon.

It blinked and might have shaken its head, but the movement was so faint that I wondered if I was making it up.

I looked at Aidan. "Do you think it understands me?"

"Hard to say." He reached out a finger, hovering it a few inches away from the dragon.

The little gray dragon hissed.

"Hey, now. He's nice," I said.

The dragon glanced at me, then at Aidan, then stretched its neck out to sniff Aidan's fingertip. A weird, deep trilling noise came from its chest, then it rubbed its head against Aidan's fingers.

"Like a cat," I murmured. "I've always wanted a cat."

"Well, you can't have my dragonets," an angry voice said.

I whipped around, searching the forest. The dragonet launched itself from my hand back into the air. I couldn't see anyone in the trees around us.

"Nullifier! We're here as friends," I said.

No response. The four dragonets flew off, disappearing between the trees. I reached for my dragon sense. It pulled me forward.

"Come on," I said. "Let's follow him."

I ran through the forest, trying to keep my footsteps light. Though he was old, from what I'd heard, the Nullifier was fast. And he knew this forest.

"We need your help," I called. "Please just talk to us!"

Golden lights sparkled in the forest around us, trying desperately to catch our attention. I kept my mind focused on the tug of my dragon sense and my gaze on the forest ahead.

Suddenly, the ground gave out from beneath my feet. I screamed, my arms pin-wheeling. I grabbed onto roots and dirt, clawing at anything I could touch to try to slow my descent. I slammed into the ground. Pain surged up my legs.

I scrambled up, but nothing felt broken. Aidan surged to his feet beside me.

Darkness all around. Light from above. Fifteen feet up, maybe twenty.

"Good trap," Aidan said.

"Yep." The walls were vertical and the tree roots too skinny to be used for climbing. "Really good trap."

Aidan walked the perimeter of the hole as I let my eyes adjust. It was about fifteen feet in diameter. A dark, deep pit perfect for sitting in while applying the lotion to its skin.

"No way out from down here," Aidan said.

"Hello!" I called up. "We're just here to chat!"

Okay, that was a lie. We were here to ask him to risk his life to save Magic's Bend. But I didn't think I should lead with that.

There was only silence from above.

"I'm Cass Clereaux," I called up. "I'm here with my friend Aidan. Your friend Aethelred sent us."

A head appeared from above. It was backlit by the sun, so I couldn't make out features, but it had to be the Nullifier.

"Aethelred?" His voice sounded creakier and older than it had.

"Yes! Aethelred. Though he appears to like the color blue better."

The figure grunted. "That he does."

"Will you let us out?" I asked.

"No way to get out," he said. "Gravity only works one way."

"A rope, maybe?"

"Why are you here?" Distrust tinged his voice. "And how'd you get past my security?"

"Your security quite liked me," I said, recalling the dragons.

The figure grunted again. "Terrible taste, those dragonets have."

"What is a dragonet?" I asked.

"A small dragon, naturally. Not flesh and blood like the old dragons, but magic. They're part of Swiss folklore."

Of course. "They're amazing."

"Flattery will get you nowhere, girl."

Damn. I'd been hoping it would. Though I had meant every word. Those dragonets *had* been amazing.

"She means it," Aidan said. "Cass doesn't lie."

Yes, I do. And he knew it.

"Who are you?" the Nullifier asked.

"Aidan Merrick."

"The Origin. Don't like your kind."

"How many could you have met?" Aidan asked.

"More than you'd expect."

"Hopefully not my father," Aidan said.

"Fortunately not. Though I've heard of him. I hope the apple falls far from the tree."

"It does." There was no offense in Aidan's voice. Not that I'd expected any, considering his father's wrongdoing. Murdering friends and colleagues was hard to come back from.

"Good, then." The Nullifier shifted so that his head disappeared. "Enjoy your stay!"

Like the freaking Holiday Inn?

"Wait!" I called. "You have to help us! Aethelred's home will be destroyed if you don't. Thousands of homes will be lost. People's lives."

An aggrieved sigh sounded from above. His head appeared a moment later.

"How can I trust you?" he asked. "If you know what I am, you understand why I must be wary."

"I do! I do understand." And could relate, considering that I, too, spent most of my life hiding. "It's smart to be wary. Call Aethelred. He'll vouch for us."

"Call him? With what? Do I look like someone who would have one of those blasted mobile telephones?"

I didn't know what he looked like, but he sure didn't sound like someone who would have anything to do with technology.

"Use my phone!"

"But then I'd have to let you out," he said. "And I don't think I'll do that. Farewell!"

His footsteps hurried away.

"Shit." I looked at Aidan. His face was cast in shadow. "Any chance you could fly us out of here?"

A second passed. Tension creased his brow. "No. My magic is still blocked by the Nullifier. I can't access my Magica or Shifter powers." He shuddered. "It feels like hell."

A sympathetic shiver crossed my skin. I tried my Mirror Mage powers again, hoping I could mirror Aidan's power over the earth and lift us out of here.

I breathed deeply and called upon my magic. I found nothing but emptiness, like a gnawing hunger. Not unexpected, but miserable.

I sank down against the dirt wall and clutched my stomach.

"This is the worst," I said.

Aidan dropped down next to me and looped an arm around my shoulders. I snuggled up against him. He smelled like himself—soap and spice—but his distinct forest scent was missing.

"I think I get why the charms comms and your healing work. They can't hurt the Nullifier. But I don't get why my FireSoul power works," I said. "I could use that against him."

"Your FireSoul power isn't like any other power. It's not really a magical talent. It probably can't be repressed by the Nullifier because it's who you are, not what you can do."

Who I was.

I didn't know if I liked the sound of that. The only example I had of FireSouls who'd embraced their nature were the Monster and the Illusionist.

The others—Nix, Del, Aaron, the FireSoul I'd gotten my lightning power from—had fought their natures.

So what did that make me?

Good? Bad? A monster?

I didn't know what I was. And it didn't really matter. My existential crisis was nothing compared to the fact that Magic's Bend was at risk.

I shook my head and scrubbed my hands over my eyes, trying to force my worry away. I had shit to do.

"Okay. We've got no magic," I said. "Just my FireSoul ability. So, I guess I'll try to find us an exit."

It was a weird use of my power, but I had to at least try. I closed my eyes and focused on my desire to escape. Maybe I'd find the perfect path of sturdy roots to climb to freedom.

But my dragon sense lay dormant.

"Nothing," I said. "There is no path. The walls are too soft, and the roots too skinny."

What the hell was my dragon side good for if it couldn't get me out of a stupid hole?

Dragons.

I leapt to my feet.

"Dragonets!" I called softly, picturing them in my mind. I tried to reach out to them mentally—something that felt a bit like hoodoo but was worth a try. "Dragonets!"

I focused everything I had on the tiny dragons, feeling like a Khaleesi-wannabe. But these dragons weren't my children, and I was no mother of dragons. I was just a girl stuck in a hole hoping that I had some ridiculous power to call dragonets to me.

"Dragonets!" I kept my voice singsong and low, trying not to alert the Nullifier. He didn't like his dragonets' affinity for me.

I glanced down at Aidan. "Is this ridiculous?"

"Best chance we—" A grin spread across his face, and he pointed up. "Not ridiculous at all."

I glanced up. Four small figures hovered at the mouth of the hole—flame, smoke, stone, and water. Their wings glinted in the light. I grinned.

"We need a way out!" I called up.

The water dragon flew down to me, hovering just out of reach. She—and I was just guessing it was a she—was the strangest and most beautiful thing I'd ever seen. Her body was transparent crystalline blue, like the Caribbean Sea. Light from above glinted off her wings, making her shimmer even in this darkness.

"Will you help me?" I asked.

She tilted her head, as if considering me, then flew back up to the light. The four dragonets raced off. Aching emptiness filled my chest. My new friends didn't actually like me.

"Guess that didn't work." I hated the lame dejection in my voice. "I can call Del to come get us, but she's still regenerating her power. It'll take a while."

Something thumped against the dirt wall next to me. I spun to see.

A thick rope lay against the wall, hanging from the hole above. The four dragonets hovered at the top of our pit.

"Holy crap," I said. "It worked."

"Up you go," Aidan said. "I'll catch you if it breaks."

His chivalry both annoyed and delighted me. But from a practical standpoint, I was lightest and least likely to break the rope. Who knew if the dragonets had tied it off to something sturdy? Physics, and knots, were probably not their strong suit. And at least one of us needed to make it out of here to help the other.

"All right, thanks," I said.

I grabbed the rope and started to climb, bracing my feet against the earthen wall. Dirt crumbled and I slipped a few times, but I made it to the top. The grass felt heavenly beneath my hands as I scrambled out of the hole.

"Thank you," I said to the dragonets.

They fluttered nearby. Acknowledging my gratitude?

I glanced around. There was no one else in the forest, just dappled sunlight and silent trees. My gaze followed the rope, finding it tied around the base of a tree. Probably the Nullifier's backup plan if he caught the wrong people.

I turned and leaned over the hole, meeting Aidan's gaze below.

"The rope is tied to something strong. You should be good to climb out."

Aidan scaled the rope like a pro, easily three times as fast as me.

"All right, let's go find that jerk," I said. "I can't believe he left us in that hole. To die?"

"Hopefully not," Aidan said. "If he's willing to let us starve to death in a pit, it's going to be damned hard to get his help."

"No kidding." I took a deep breath and focused on my dragon sense. The tug about my middle pulled me left.

"That way. We're actually close now." I turned to the dragonets. "Thank you again."

They stared back at me. I decided to assume they understood.

Aidan and I set off through the forest. The dragonets trailed behind. I could get used to these little shadows. It'd make going out in human cities difficult, but I'd be willing to adjust.

A few minutes later, we came across a quaint cottage sitting in a small clearing. It looked a lot like the one from Sleeping Beauty, so idyllic that it outshone even Stechelberg. There was even a little water wheel churning up the stream that flowed by the house. Flowers in a riot of shades tumbled from window boxes and along the edges of the house.

"Looks like our guy is a gardener."

The front door opened. A small, white-haired man in a tweed suit peered out, shock on his face. He reminded me a lot of Dr. G. There were even leather patches at his elbows.

"How'd you get out?" Irritation colored his demand.

I pointed back to the dragonets. "Had a little help."

He scowled at the dragonets. "Traitors."

"Don't blame them," I said. "I can be very persuasive."

His blue gaze met mine, considering. "How? They don't like anyone but me. And even me they aren't sure of."

I shrugged. It was probably my FireSoul they liked, but I wasn't going to share that. Considering the hell my FireSoul had put me through, it was nice to have a sweet perk like being friends with tiny dragons.

"We still need your help," I said.

"I left you in a pit. How did that not convince you I'm not willing to help?" he said.

"We don't have a choice," I said. "You're our last hope to save Magic's Bend. An enormous portal is out of control. It's going to destroy the town. Thousands of people will lose their lives."

He harrumphed. "Not my problem."

"But it could be," Aidan said. "You could be a hero."

"Or at least not an asshole," I said. "Because it takes a real asshole to ignore this kind of thing."

The Nullifier's eyes flared wide. He harrumphed again. And again. Like he didn't know what to say. I wondered how many people he'd spoken to in the years he'd been hiding. Not many, if those booby-traps were anything to go by.

He turned to go into his house. "Come in, then."

I glanced at Aidan and gave a small fist pump, then followed the Nullifier into his house.

It was bigger on the inside than I'd expected, and just as quaint as the outside. Dark wood chairs with brightly colored cushions crouched around an iron fireplace. All old and homemade, but well cared for. Cuckoo clocks lined the walls. There was nothing modern within, but I wasn't surprised.

The Nullifier stood and looked around. His dilemma was clear. There were only two chairs in front of the fire.

"Go through." The Nullifier gestured to a door at the back of the house before going into another room. "I will bring tea."

"Now we get tea?" I mouthed at Aidan.

He shrugged, then walked toward the back door. I followed him out into a small garden. A delicate, wrought-iron patio set graced the flagstone seating area. Flowers in every shade of the rainbow edged the patio. A meadow extended about fifty yards, terminating at the forest.

Aidan and I sat. A few minutes later, the Nullifier came out with a delicate porcelain tea set and joined us.

I reached for a white teacup painted with pink and blue flowers. "Thank you." My eyes landed on the small plate of chocolate. "Chocolate?"

"This is Switzerland."

I took a piece of chocolate, unable to help myself. "Do you have a name?"

"None that need concern you."

"All right." I hesitated. "I guess I'll just call you the Nullifier, then."

"Fine. Now tell me what is wrong. I cannot say that I will help, but I will listen. It's the least I can do for someone who has gained the approval of the dragonets."

"Can I ask how you found them?" I always figured it was smart to spend a few minutes of fostering good will by showing interest in the person you wanted something from. And I was genuinely interested.

"I didn't. They found me. They live here, in this forest. They protect me because they have grown to like me."

"Really? I thought dragons had died out."

He shrugged. "They may have. Like I said, these are not flesh and blood dragons, but magic. Though there is folklore that says dragons used to live in these mountains. Some believe they still do."

Real dragons, swooping amongst the dramatic peaks that surrounded us? My heart lightened at the idea, warmth flowing through my chest. I'd love to see that.

"Is that why you settled here?" I asked.

"No. I settled here because it is remote and there are no nearby magical settlements." He sipped his tea. "Now what do you need help with?"

I set my teacup down and told him about the portal and Magic's Bend. Gravity settled over his features as he listened.

"And so we were hoping you could come through the portal with us and disenchant the Pool of Enchantment. Then, we could get rid of the portal for good."

He leaned back in his chair. "Well, that is terrible. But I cannot come."

"You can't?" I almost shrieked the words. I couldn't believe he was willing to let Magic's Bend be destroyed.

"I do not leave my home. Considering that you need help far away, it is impossible."

Birds chirped in the distance, their song somehow piercing the roar of rage in my head. This guy had the chance to save a whole city and he wasn't going to take it?

"That is my final say in the matter," the Nullifier said.

I opened my mouth to respond, but my skin prickled with unease, a strange feeling that was totally out of place with my anger. The sense of foreboding wouldn't abate. I glanced at Aidan. His brow was creased.

Beyond him, the forest trees seemed to shimmer. I sucked in a breath, getting a hint of a strange smell. Dark magic? But I had to be imagining it. The Nullifier would crush any magic before it could even approach. He'd created a bubble, a no-magic zone.

The birds went silent.

My spine stiffened. I reached for my magic but found nothing. The Nullifier's doing. So I moved my hand toward the daggers at my thighs.

"There's something—"

An explosion blew my world apart, deafening me. It blasted me through the air. I crashed to the ground, my head ringing and my eyes blind. I lay stunned, gasping.

Cool water brushed over my face, clearing my head.

I blinked, my vision slowly returning. The water dragonet hovered above me. I scrambled to my feet. The yard was chaos. The flagstone patio had been blown apart by some magical concussive force. Rocks and dirt scattered all around. Flowers were everywhere.

A dozen yards away, Aidan stumbled to his feet. The Nullifier lay on the other side of the yard, still. The magical void I'd felt ever since trying to access my magic lifted. Did that mean the Nullifier was dead?

Please no.

With him died our hope of saving Magic's Bend.

Suddenly, demons crashed through the trees, charging us. Their gray forms bulged with muscle, and their horns swept back along their skulls.

Shadow demons.

Fear tasted metallic in my mouth. These were the demons that the Monster most commonly used as his henchmen. But if they were here for me, how the hell did they find me?

One demon raised an arm and threw a blast of smoke. It hurtled through the air, a gray cloud that I knew to be blazing hot and propelled by the force of a locomotive.

I lunged, throwing myself to the grass and barely escaping the searing heat that would have plowed me into the ground and probably knocked me unconscious.

As I scrambled to my feet, Aidan threw a huge jet of flame, bowling over three demons. Their gray bodies flew back, two of them smashing into the trees. The pines snapped and careened backward.

Aidan's magic appeared to be unlocked too.

I drew upon my own, calling up my lightning and letting it crackle and burn beneath my skin. Warmth and joy surged as it unfurled in my chest. Now that I'd embraced my magic, using it was bliss. Like I was fully complete. How had I lived so long without this? Like I'd been half of myself.

When I'd formed a big enough bolt, I threw it at two demons who were only ten yards away. Thunder cracked, nearly deafening, as it hurtled through the air and struck their hulking forms. They stopped dead in their tracks, their bodies jerking as they collapsed.

More demons spilled from the forest. Aidan threw fire, his jets so precisely aimed that they killed the demons without lighting up the trees and grass. I shot lightning, picking them off as they charged. Thunder boomed, an eerie sound on such a cloudless, perfect day. My skin felt electrified. I reveled in it.

Aidan and I made a good team. He was wasted as a millionaire business owner. Fighting was his strength.

The dragonets streaked from around the house, their small bodies hurtling toward the demons. Glittering blue, blazing red, deep dark brown, and ethereal gray all charged toward the threat to avenge their friend, the Nullifier.

The fire dragonet collided with a demon, lighting him up in an inferno of flame. The water dragonet quickly doused the blaze. I winced, thinking of the immense heat and then deadly cold of the water dragonet. The stone dragonet threw itself into a demon, the blow so hard that the demon flew off his feet and through the air, colliding with a tree.

But the worst was the smoke dragonet. He flew straight at the face of the demon nearest me, disappearing inside of him. The demon's eyes widened, horrified, as he convulsed and collapsed.

Possession by smoke dragonet? No thanks. Especially since the shadow demon seemed to be suffocating from within, from the look of the smoke billowing from his mouth and nose. I shuddered, then turned back to the forest, ready to electrocute more demons.

What I saw made my knees weaken.

The Monster.

He strolled from the forest, calm as could be, his suit so perfectly pressed he looked like he represented a Swiss bank. His dull brown gaze was bland.

I drew in a ragged breath, suddenly unable to remember any of my powers.

CHAPTER ELEVEN

Aidan stood between the Monster and me. His head whipped toward the Nullifier. A silver gray light swirled around Aidan until the massive golden griffin stood in his place. He crouched low, then launched himself in the air.

I steadied my breathing, forcing myself to remember my magic, and called upon a bolt of lightning. When it crackled beneath my skin, I launched it at the Monster. Thunder boomed as it hurtled toward him.

The Monster threw up a hand. My lightning ricocheted off the barrier he'd created, bouncing straight back to me. I lunged out of the path of fiery light, skidding in the dirt as it streaked overhead and plowed into a corner of the Nullifier's house.

I scrambled to my feet as Aidan swooped down from above, landing with a thud next to me. I met his dark gaze, understanding, and gripped his soft fur in my hands, then scrambled onto his back, settling in behind his wings.

His magic washed over me, the scent of forest so strong it smelled like I was in a Christmas tree. The sound of crashing waves drowned out the Monster's enraged shout. Aidan crouched low, then launched himself into the air. Wind tore at my hair as we hurtled upward. I gathered up my lightning to shoot at the Monster, though I knew he would likely deflect it.

"Get the Nullifier!" I shouted at Aidan as I aimed my bolt.

Aidan turned from the Monster and flew toward the Nullifier, who still lay on the ground. I twisted on his back to keep the Monster in sight. The dragonets were charging the Monster, their little forms glittering in the sunlight.

"No! Dragonets! No!" They were no match for the Monster.

I hurled my bolt of lightning, distracting the Monster from the dragonets. The dragonets watched the Monster deflect the bolt, then turned and flew toward me. My heart soared.

The Monster raised a hand and threw an enormous jet of fire at us. Aidan couldn't see it, of course.

"Left!" I screamed at Aidan.

I gripped his fur as he dodged left, but the flame ignited his wing. The smell of burning feathers singed my nose. The water dragonet sped forward, throwing itself against Aidan's wing. The dragonet exploded in a burst of water, droplets flying everywhere.

"No!" I reached for the dragonet. I didn't want Aidan to be burned, but I also didn't want the dragonet to die.

The flames extinguished and the water flew through the air, as if in rewind, and formed back into the shape of the water dragonet.

A victory laugh escaped me as Aidan plunged toward the ground and the collapsed form of the Nullifier. I prayed that he was still alive.

As gently as if he were picking up a kitten, the griffin's enormous claws curled around the Nullifier and lifted him into the air. I twisted around to see the Monster raising his hand to throw another blast of magic at us.

But Aidan was so fast that we were a hundred yards away in seconds. I was about to pull the transportation stone from my pocket and get us the hell out of Switzerland when the Nullifier shouted from his place resting in Aidan's claws.

I leaned over to look down at him, catching sight of his panicked gaze darting from the Monster on the ground below to the griffin above him. Less than a second later, the magic that had flared to life in my chest died, replaced by the now familiar aching loss that accompanied the Nullifier using his powers.

Dread had only a millisecond to set up camp in my heart when the griffin beneath me disappeared. I screamed as we plummeted through the air, me, Aidan in his human form, and the Nullifier.

Before his magic had been nullified, Aidan had flown us out over a deep valley. The ground was thousands of feet below.

"Stop!" I screamed at the Nullifier, my gasping shout lost on the wind that tore at my clothes and made my eyes water. My stomach was in my chest, and my hands clawed at the air.

The little dragonets swooped around us helplessly, too small to lift us.

The Nullifier's panicked gaze met my own.

"Stop!" I screamed.

A massive concussive force bowled into me, knocking the breath from my lungs. The Monster had thrown one of his signature sonic booms. Pain bloomed in my entire body. Before my vision darkened, I caught sight of the Nullifier pin-wheeling through the sky. He must have been hit with the majority of the boom. The Monster had hit me with one once. It'd made my insides feel like soup.

When I opened my eyes again, we were still falling, though much closer to the ground. I'd only been out a second.

My magic bloomed in my chest. Hope swelled. I prayed the Nullifier wasn't dead, but the fact that I had my magic meant that maybe I wouldn't be crushed to death on the valley floor. Aidan would have his magic too. And he could fly.

I twisted my head, looking for Aidan. I caught sight of him twenty yards away, falling through the air. Silver gray light surrounded him, the most beautiful thing I'd ever seen. The wind tore at my hair and clothes as I plummeted, and I prayed Aidan would be in time. I glanced at the ground. It was closer, but still far.

Maybe this would work.

A golden blur caught my gaze. I looked up to see the griffin, fully transformed. He swooped under me, catching me on his back. Relief welled. Not enough to banish the fear, but enough to get me moving.

I clutched his warm fur gratefully and scrambled high onto his back. He flew left, then plunged again, right beneath the Nullifier. I reached out and grabbed onto the Nullifier's tweed coat, then dragged him onto Aidan's back. In the distance, the dragonets flew off, I hoped toward safety.

I pulled his unconscious body close, my stomach still in my throat as we surged upward, the griffin's powerful wings beating the air. I was *so* not built for this kind of travel.

I dug into my pocket and withdrew the transport charm.

"I'm throwing the transport charm!" I shouted at Aidan.

I thought his head nodded, so I chucked the stone ahead of us and envisioned the safest place I could think of. The stone exploded in a poof of silver dust, and the griffin hurtled into it.

A second later, we soared over the green fields of Ireland, Aidan's massive estate below. It was the only house for miles, and the emerald hills rolled out in every direction.

The griffin headed for the front lawn and slowed its descent to land gracefully on the grass.

I scrambled off his back, trying to carefully bring the Nullifier's body with me. I crashed to my butt, but I kept the Nullifier from further injury.

The ground had never felt so good.

I resisted the urge to kiss it and felt for the Nullifier's pulse instead. His skin felt paper thin beneath my fingertips. He must be ancient.

There!

Faint, but definitely there. In a swirl of silver light, Aidan transformed back into a man.

"We need to get in the house." Aidan swept the Nullifier into his arms and sprinted across the grass. I surged to my feet and followed.

We raced up the sweeping stairs to the front door. A gust of wind forced the door open with a bang. Aidan's elemental powers, I realized. I raced into the foyer behind Aidan and shut the door, panting.

"The house is guarded," Aidan said as he took the grand stairs two at a time. "I think the Nullifier's powers broke your concealment charm. As long as you're near him, the Monster can find you. But if he's passed out, your concealment charm and the protections on the house will hold. You should be safe."

For magic's sake, I'd never even thought of that. I was losing my edge.

I ran up the stairs behind Aidan, following him to the first bedroom on the left. He laid the Nullifier on the grand bed, then pressed his hands to his shoulders.

Aidan's magic surged on the air as he fed healing power into the Nullifier. The old man's color improved slightly—less of a deadly pale, at least.

"Dial zero on the phone near the bed," Aidan said. "Tell Iona to get the closest healer here now."

Iona was the housekeeper, I recalled. I'd been here once before, and she'd made a delicious dinner, though

I'd never met her. My fingers trembled as I dialed the phone. I blurted the request when she picked up. She didn't even bother asking who I was, just said the healer would be here straightaway. I hung up.

"How's he doing?" I approached Aidan and stared down at the Nullifier's still form. Though his color had slightly improved, his cheeks looked sunken, and his breath was shallow. I had to squint to even tell if his chest was moving.

"Still alive," Aidan said. "But that sonic boom hit him dead on. At his age, he's lucky he didn't die on the spot. Another hit like that and he'd have been dead."

This had been the trauma that Aethelred had mentioned. Time and decay might not get the Nullifier, but murder could.

"You could have shifted in the air, Cass." Censure laced his tone. "I like saving you, but you need to remember your powers. You could have mirrored my ability to shift and saved yourself. What if I hadn't gotten to you in time?"

He was right. Damn it. I'd been so freaked out by falling that I hadn't even thought of it. The idea that I might have let myself be pancaked because I hadn't remembered all my powers made me cringe.

I scrubbed a weary hand over my face. "You're right. I need to be better at it."

He nodded. "Good. You're powerful, but you need to be faster."

I studied the floorboards hard, disappointed in myself. I was learning. But he was right, there wasn't time for me to do it slowly.

A few moments later, a banging sounded at the front door.

"I'll get it." I left Aidan to continue trying to heal the Nullifier and sprinted down the stairs, grateful to be on my own with my embarrassment. I peered through the wavy glass inset in the door. "Who is it?"

"Healer Caerdowen," a feminine voice said. "Called by Iona."

I didn't feel any dark magic wafting through the door, so I pulled it open. A pretty woman with serious eyes stood on the other side. She was dressed like a mountain climber in cargo pants and an athletic t-shirt, but there was an old-fashioned doctor's bag gripped in her hand. I stepped back to let her enter, then shut the door.

"Come on," I said. "He's up here."

"What am I dealing with?" she asked as she hurried up the stairs beside me.

"Sonic boom hit an old man."

"How old?"

"No idea. Older than is natural. He's got some protection against aging."

"All right, then."

We hurried into the room. Aidan stepped aside as Caerdowen approached. She studied the Nullifier, her gaze serious.

I stood near Aidan and gripped his hand, comforted by his warmth and strength.

"Do you think he'll be all right?" I asked.

"Give me a moment." Caerdowen's tone was all business. It comforted me. This chick could handle herself and whatever her job threw at her.

I stood in anxious silence. When I was unable to take it any longer, I leaned up and whispered to Aidan, "I'm going to go call Aerdeca and see how the museum is doing."

He nodded and leaned down to kiss my forehead. A small burst of heat flared inside me. I ignored it and hurried from the room, pulling my cellphone out of my pocket.

The battery was almost dead, but it should do. I found Aerdeca's name in my contacts and pressed *Call.*

"Do you have any answers?" she demanded as soon as she picked up.

"Maybe. We'll know soon." *If our savior is alive or dead.* "How is the museum?"

"Still glowing and disappearing. More of the east wing has disappeared, but the majority is still there."

My shoulders slumped in relief. We still had time. At this rate of disappearance, a whole day. Maybe even two. Not that we'd wait that long. We needed to fix the portal ASAP.

"How is Mordaca?" I asked. "And the rest?"

"The same. Frozen. She's alive though."

"Good. We'll be back soon. I think we've got an answer. But has the Order of the Magica said anything?"

"They're trying to find a Nullifier. They had one other lead, but they didn't sound confident."

How many Nullifiers could there be? Surely more than one. Or maybe not. Either way, I needed to pray that our Nullifier recovered. For his own sake and for ours.

"That's all they've got?" I asked.

"Apparently this is unusual," Aerdeca said.

"No kidding. I'll be in touch." I hung up the phone and returned to the room.

The healer stepped back from the bed and turned. "I put a quick-healing spell on him. He'll sleep for about seven or eight hours and wake in good health."

Seven or eight hours? Did we have seven or eight hours? I thought so, though it didn't really matter because we didn't have much choice.

"Thank you," Aidan said. "What should we do for him in the meantime?"

"Have someone sit with him to monitor his progress, but he should be fine."

"Excellent. Thank you for your help. Please send the bill to Iona."

She nodded and departed. Aidan went to the phone and dialed. From his words, I guessed he was asking Iona to come watch the Nullifier.

When he hung up, I said, "So now what?"

"Now, we have our date." His gray gaze was serious.

I laughed. "Our date?"

"We've got seven or eight hours. We can get some solid dating in. And I'm going to try, because I've accepted the fact that you don't have a normal schedule. Restaurant and a movie may never happen, so we're going to get creative."

"I don't like movie theaters all that much anyway," I said. My heart beat frantically, like a butterfly on speed. I was tired from all we'd been through, but at least I wasn't sick or injured. I could definitely get on board with whatever Aidan had planned.

"What are we going to do?" I asked.

"We'll shower first. Then I'll get us food."

"What?" I gestured up and down my body, at the blood and dirt and singe marks. I could literally not remember the last time I'd showered. "You don't like this?"

"Oh, I like it." His gaze heated. "You can stay just like that if you want. But I'm going to shower."

I grinned. "All right. I'll meet you after. Where, though?"

"There's a room at the end of the east wing on the second floor. Take your time. I'll bring us dinner there."

"Deal," I said.

"I'll wait with the Nullifier until Iona shows. You can get started."

"What, you think I'll need extra time?" I lifted a tangled, dirty hunk of my hair and showed it off.

He laughed. "Just go."

I grinned and left, passing Iona in the hall as I made my way to the guest bedroom I'd used last time I was here. I greeted her briefly, then hurried on.

As I entered the opulent suite—all modern luxury, unlike Aidan's more traditional home in Magic's Bend—I pressed the comms charm at my neck to turn it on.

"Del? Nix?" I asked.

"Hey," Nix said.

"Yo," Del said.

"Del, you think you'll be ready to take us through the portal in seven or eight hours?"

"Just about," Del said. "It's not too long of a journey, so I should be okay."

"Great, thank you. How're you? And Dr. Garriso?"

"We're good," Nix said. "So is Dr. Garriso. He's up and about now."

"Good," I said. I considered telling them about my date, but discarded the idea. I wanted to get to the date sooner, not spend my seven hours talking about it. They could get the news later. "Be safe there, okay? I'll call you before we leave here."

"Sure thing. You too," Del said.

"Seconded," Nix said.

"Bye, guys." I grinned as I disconnected the comms charm and walked into the bathroom. I turned toward the mirror and almost shrieked.

A banshee stared back at me, wild red hair sticking out at all angles and coated in dirt and grass. My eyes were wild and my skin streaked with blood and more dirt. I was pretty much ninety percent dirt with speckles of blood.

Aidan wanted to date me like this?

I grinned and shrugged, then headed to the enormous shower to turn on the water. If Aidan wanted to be my dude, he'd probably better get used to me being filthy. True, I was presently grosser than normal. My usual jobs only involved forty percent dirt coverage, at most.

But best to begin as you intend to continue, someone smarter than me once said.

I turned the fancy silver taps in the big marble shower and jumped back as the eight shower heads turned on. My laugh echoed off the gleaming stone walls, and I made quick work of stripping out of my clothes. They were so filthy that they almost stood up on their own.

It didn't take me long to get clean, but I spent an extra few minutes because the shower was just plain awesome. It was one of my favorite places in the world. I'd dreamed of it since I'd used it last, every time I'd stepped into my own tiny one at home.

Regretfully, I climbed out of the shower and gazed dourly at my filthy clothes. I really didn't want to put them on like that. Maybe Aidan had clothes in the closet in this room. I went out to check, but my gaze was caught by the note and clothes on the bed.

It was short, saying only that I could toss my dirty clothes in the washer in the room at the end of the hall, and Iona would see that they made it to the dryer. There was a big t-shirt and gym shorts next to the note on the bed.

Aidan's.

They didn't fit, but they were clean, and that was all I cared about. I tugged them on, then carried my dirty clothes to the washroom and loaded the state-of-the art washer.

"Could probably fly to the moon in that thing," I muttered.

My own washer bounced itself across my tiny kitchen every time I turned it on, pissing off Nix, who lived below me. Whenever I was peeved with her, I ran it at night. She retaliated by roasting broccoli, which tasted delicious but smelled vile when it wafted up through the floor. Of course, she didn't share, so I just got the smell.

We might not be blood sisters, but that didn't stop us from acting like it. And I loved her with all my heart.

After flicking off the lights in the washroom, it didn't take me long to find the room at the end of the east wing. I stepped inside, expecting a regular old sitting room and getting a masterpiece of windows and a glass ceiling instead.

Telescopes perched around the perimeter of the room, aimed at the sky. In the middle was a blanket laid out on the floor with candles and plates of sandwiches spread upon it. The dim light was enough to illuminate the scene but not kill the glow of the moon and stars sparkling through the glass above.

Aidan stood and spread out his arms. "What do you think? Not a half bad picnic."

"Not at all." It was downright perfect, in fact. "Best I've ever seen, actually."

"Iona is busy, so I had to figure out dinner on the fly. I hope sandwiches and beer are all right."

"Perfect." I approached him, my heart feeling somehow light and heavy at once.

"You look good." His dark gaze was appreciative.

I glanced down at the baggy clothes. "These old things? Just had them lying around."

He grinned, then leaned down. I stood on my tiptoes, my heart racing, and pressed my lips to his. I sighed against his mouth, at the amazing heat and softness of his lips. When he pulled away, I frowned.

"Eat," he said. "It's been too long since we've taken a break. You need to eat."

My stomach grumbled then, as if it had ears.

Aidan grinned. "See, your stomach agrees."

"Apparently." I picked up a sandwich stuffed full of ham and cheese.

Aidan popped the tops on two green glass bottles of Harp, an Irish beer I recognized from back home. It was more similar to my beloved PBR than the more famous Guinness, so I was grateful. He passed one over, and I took it gratefully and sipped the bubbling cold brew.

"So you like astronomy?" I nodded to the telescopes.

"Yeah. I used to look at the stars a lot when I was a kid stuck at my dad's place."

My heart tugged for him at the memory of the place his father had retreated to after killing two of his colleagues on the Alpha Council. Remote and desolate in the Highlands of Scotland, it would have been a lonely place for a boy to grow up.

"So now you can really look at them," I said.

He grinned. "Exactly. I rarely do, though. I ought to start."

"You should."

"I've just been so busy with Origin Enterprises." He took a bite of his sandwich, his gaze thoughtful. After he swallowed, he said, "And now with you. But that, I like."

"Me too." I sipped my beer.

"Is your locket from your parents?" he asked.

I reached up to touch the golden heart that nestled next to my comms charm, my heart pinging. "Yes. At least, I think so. I want it to be from them."

"There's nothing inside of it?" he asked. "No photos?"

"I can't open it." I'd tried a lot as a girl, hoping to find a clue about my past within. "It's stuck."

"You've tried magic?"

"I have, but not much. Just took it to a couple of witches when I was a teenager. They couldn't get it open." Hope flared in my chest. "But maybe Aethelred can help. I'm going to see him about it as soon as we fix the portal."

"It's a good idea."

We finished eating, chatting about lighter topics than dead parents and lonely childhoods. I felt like I'd known Aidan longer than I actually had, as if the dramatic nature of our circumstance drew us closer. But that was pretty textbook, right?

"Would you like to look at the stars?" Aidan asked.

"Sure." This was turning out to be a really good date.

We found spots at the side of the room and lay on our backs, an enormous telescope propped over us and pointing at the glass ceiling. Aidan was so close that the heat of his body warmed mine, sending goosebumps over my skin.

This was the first time in a month that we'd been alone and not running for out lives or one of us ill from injuries. Which made it damned hard to focus on Aidan's words as he told me how to adjust the telescope.

His arm brushed my chest as he fiddled with the telescope, trying to give me the best view of the stars or planets or whatever the hell I was supposed to be looking at.

"There," he said, his voice low at my ear. "Now you can look."

I peered up through the telescope, trying to focus on the lights and colors, but all I could comprehend was Aidan's soft breath at my ear and the touch of his arm against mine.

When I felt his hand on my stomach, I stiffened, my heart pounding a fierce tattoo against my ribs. He paused, his hand warm and still, as if to give me a chance to protest.

I didn't. I just stayed staring up through the telescope, praying he'd move his hand up or down or anywhere at all.

When he drew his fingertips in circles on my abdomen, my breathing became harsher.

"You're so damned beautiful, Cass." His voice was a rasp at my ear.

I shivered, then tilted my face toward his for a kiss.

"Keep looking," he said.

I almost growled, but the promise in his eyes made me turn my head back to the telescope. When I'd finally focused back on the star or planet—I had no idea because I'd been distracted when he'd described what I was looking at—Aidan's fingertips drifted beneath my shirt.

They were hot against my stomach, a burning brand so fierce it might leave a mark. Tingles streaked through me, lighting up all my nerve endings and making me whimper.

A satisfied sound escaped Aidan's throat, the closest thing to a growl I'd ever heard a human make. When his lips pressed to my throat, I closed my eyes, giving up on the stars above. I focused only on the path of his lips and the pleasure that trailed behind.

His tongue darted out, licking a delicate line along the tendon at my neck. My breath strangled in my lungs, and my head spun. It'd been ages since I'd been with a guy, and this wasn't any guy.

This was Aidan.

The guy.

My guy.

The one that I'd gotten to know so well, that I respected so much. Having waited for this, instead of making it a quick hookup between jobs, made it so much more special.

Not to mention hot. I was on fire, every part of my body blazing like an inferno. I might not be ready to round all the bases yet, but I didn't want to stop here, either.

Unable to take it anymore, I turned and met his gaze. "I'm done looking at the stars."

CHAPTER TWELVE

In some wonderful twist of fate, I woke before our alarm clock, nestled against Aidan's side. I yawned, memories of last night sending heat across my cheeks. We hadn't gone all the way—I hadn't been ready yet—but what we'd done had given me more than enough reason to turn red from my head to my toes.

The dawn sun broke through the clouds on the horizon and sent a golden light into the bedroom. It reflected off Aidan's face, highlighting his ridiculous hotness and the dark sweep of his lashes. His lips were still slightly swollen, and I blushed at the memory of the things he'd done with them.

As if he'd sensed my thoughts, his eyes opened. He blinked sleepily, then turned his head toward me.

"Hey." Sleep roughened his voice.

"Hey."

"Thanks for last night," he said.

"Likewise." I kissed his lips, then shivered again. "You did most of the work."

"I'd hardly call it work." He grinned. "But if you're hiring, consider last night my application."

"You're on the payroll." I wished we could stay here all morning. My body ached, and my brain was still foggy from sleep. We hadn't gotten much rest last night, but it'd been enough to get me ready to go today.

The reminder of what faced us cast a pall over my cheer.

"We should go see the Nullifier. He should wake soon," I said.

"You're right." Aidan leaned over and kissed me one last time, then we both hurried out of bed.

Aidan fetched my clean clothes from the washroom—I'd refused to do the walk of shame through his house in case Iona was in the hall—while I brushed my teeth in the bathroom.

After dressing, I grabbed my cell phone from the bedside table. As I went to shove it into my pocket, the blinking blue light caught my eye. I turned it over to look at the screen.

Missed Call.

From Aerdeca.

Oh shit.

I stabbed her name with my thumb and hit *Call*, then waited, bouncing on my feet.

"You need to get here quick," she said as soon as the line connected.

"What's wrong?"

"More than half the museum is gone now. And the portal has expanded even more. The Order thinks it could suck in more than Magic's Ben. Maybe as far as Portland."

Where my friends were.

185

"Shit. Okay. We're coming. Be there within an hour." I prayed I could deliver that. I'd only be able to if the Nullifier woke up.

I hung up with Aerdeca and found the Nullifier's room. Aidan was already there, talking to Iona's niece, who had taken over for her in the middle of last night.

"I'll bring breakfast here," she said, her Irish accent a charming match to her red curls. My *deirfiúr* and I had trained ourselves away from our accents as a way to better hide our real identities, but I'd probably sound and look just as wholesomely Irish as Siobhán if I hadn't.

"Thank you, Siobhán," Aidan said.

She grinned and left the room.

"He needs to wake up soon," I murmured as we sat in the chairs at the side of his bed. As much as I wanted to shake him awake, he was old and healing, and even I wasn't that big of a jerk.

As I told Aidan about the conversation with Aerdeca, I couldn't stop bouncing my knee as I watched the Nullifier, hoping his eyes would open.

When they finally did, part of me regretted hoping they'd open. As soon as his gaze landed on us, my magic dampened. The aching loss filled my chest. He had to be dampening the magic that fueled my concealment charm as well.

"Stop," I pleaded. "You'll lead the Monster to us."

The Nullifier's blue gaze cleared. His dampening power dissipated. My shoulders relaxed as my magic welled again, filling the emptiness in my chest.

"How did he find me after all these years?" he asked, his gaze both worried and curious.

"What? Who?"

"Victor Orriordor. The man who walked into the clearing at my home and then blew me out of the sky."

"Victor Orriordor?" My heart pounded. That was the Monster's name?

"Yes. At least, that is what he used to go by. Centuries ago. But I don't understand why he found me. I thought he'd stopped looking."

"Centuries?" I was so lost. "How is he immortal?"

"I do not know. He may not be, but he's lived long somehow." The Nullifier struggled to sit upright. I helped him, adjusting the pillows behind his back.

"How did you meet him?" I asked.

"He came to me about three hundred years ago. He wanted to kill me to take my powers."

"For immortality?"

"I think not. He had the air of someone with tragedy in their past. And I'd heard stories. I thought he wanted to kill his own magic. To destroy the FireSoul within him by taking my power of nullification. It would suppress all of his magical ability. Take it away."

I cringed. Who would do that willingly to themselves? It felt like dying. I didn't like everything about being a FireSoul, but I'd *never* cut out my magic like that. Repressing it all those years had been bad enough, but at least I'd had my magic still within me, ready to access when I needed it.

Permanently killing my magic? It'd be almost worse than death.

"What happened?" I breathed.

"I fought him. Used my power to nullify his powers. It gave him a taste of what was to come, and he hesitated. I won that battle and ran, though I thought he might seek me again."

"But he never came for you?" I knew I needed to be getting his help with the portal—and I would—but this was the first opportunity I'd ever had to learn about the Monster who hunted me. The Nullifier could have the ammunition I needed to destroy the Monster and save myself.

"Not until today," the Nullifier said. "I thought he'd given up on that. I heard that he had become addicted to the power, the way FireSouls always do."

Always do.

It's not true, I wanted to cry. *I'm not addicted. I've been fighting it. I've been winning!*

Instead, I said, "So that is why you recognized him."

"Yes. Thank you for getting me away from him. But how did he find me?"

"He didn't. He found me," I said. "I had a concealment charm that protected me from him. He's been searching for me."

"Ah, yes." The Nullifier nodded. "If he had seers scrying for you, they would have found you when you entered my no-magic zone. Concealment charms are dangerous. They can hide a person from my protections. Your charm failed when you neared my home."

"But you're not using your powers now," I said. "It's the only way we're safe."

"Yes."

"And you'll help us close the portal?"

His gaze darkened.

"Victor Orriordor is behind it," I said. "If the portal devours the museum, it will kill people. Destroy thousands of homes."

"Like my home," the Nullifier said grimly.

I thought of the explosive blast that had destroyed so much of his patio and part of the back of his house. "Yes."

"Yes. I will do it," he grumbled. "Victor Orriordor is dangerous. Whatever he wants with the museum, I do not want him to have."

The tension in my shoulders loosened a bit. "Thank you!"

"Don't thank me," he groused. "We haven't succeeded yet."

We met Nix and Del on the front lawn of the museum thirty minutes later, after the Nullifier had recovered enough to be up and about. It was a bright, clear day. The kind that would have lots of kids out playing on the lawns, if half the town hadn't been enveloped in a glowing purple portal. Nix and Del stood at the edge of the Museum lawn, on a small patch that wasn't enclosed in the portal, which expanded out far in the other direction.

Most of the museum had disappeared. When it all disappeared, the imbalance in the magical power grid would cause a vacuum and destroy the town.

"It's way worse," I said as soon as I reached Nix and Del. I'd raced ahead, leaving Aidan and the Nullifier to catch up.

"Yep." Del eyed the figures behind me. "And that's our best hope?"

I glanced back at the Nullifier. I was worried about getting him through the unknown challenges at the waypoint, but we'd cross that bridge when we came to it. Or swim that ocean, or cross that desert.

"Want me to conjure a life vest?" Nix whispered, her gaze on the Nullifier. "Because if we get dumped in the ocean again, he doesn't look like the strongest swimmer."

I eyed the Nullifier, who was looking immensely better than he had earlier, but still frail. I'd seen plenty of folks over seventy swimming laps in the cold waters of the Pacific, so I knew they could be tough, but after the Nullifier's injuries, I was worried for him.

"Thanks," I said. "I wish we had any other choice because I hate asking him to do this, but we're out of options."

On a whim, I'd asked the Nullifier if he could just use his power to kill the portal from here. Unfortunately, he'd said no. The Pool of Enchantment was too powerful. He needed to kill the source of the power in order to kill the portal.

Before we'd come, Aidan had called the Order of the Magica, who had been no real help, so this was what we were going with. The Order had already sent in two contingents of their strongest Magica—two groups of six—to attempt to disenchant the pool, but neither had reported back with success. They hadn't reported back at all, actually, and the Magica were concerned they were dead or permanently lost. They were going to send another contingent in shortly after us, though I wasn't convinced they'd do any better a job.

Aerdeca approached us from across the lawn, her white suit now dingy and grass-stained. She really hadn't left her sister's side.

"I'm coming with you," Aerdeca said

I glanced at Del. "Can you take one more?"

Del shook her head. "The four of you are already a stretch. I don't think I can do another. Not if I want to have enough power to get us all back."

"I'm sorry," I told Aerdeca. "But thank you for the offer."

She twisted her hands, her normally unflappable facade clearly flapped.

"Are we all ready to go?" Aidan asked. "I don't like the look of the portal. If we're caught when the museum disappears and the portal finally closes, we could be stuck."

"I am." I glanced at the Nullifier. "Are you?"

He nodded, his gaze resolute.

"How do we do this, then?" I asked.

"Link hands," Del said. "On my count, step through. Then you lead us to the Pool of Enchantment."

I nodded. We'd told the Nullifier that I was a Seeker, which was how I'd find the Pool of Enchantment. He'd seemed to buy it, though there wasn't much reason to doubt it.

"Let's get this show on the road, then." I stepped up and took Del's hand, then linked my other with Aidan's.

I glanced at him, glad he was at my side. He gave me a half-grin that I chose to interpret as him feeling the same.

Del reached out for Nix, who then grasped the Nullifier's palm in her other hand.

"Thank you for doing this," Aerdeca said.

"Don't have much choice," I said.

"You do. None of your loved ones are trapped in that portal." Her tortured gaze traveled to Mordaca, who still floated within the purple haze.

"Ready?" I asked Del, my gaze on the purple glow that was only a foot away. My heart thudded as my mind raced over what we could be stepping into.

"Yep. On three."

I squeezed Aidan's hand.

"One, two, three!"

I stepped forward, my eyes closed and my breath caught in my chest. When I opened my eyes, we stood in the desert again, confirming my fear that this was where the Monster's home was located. The desert was like the base for this place, the absence of anything but sand and heat making it a perfect palate for the other worlds to be projected upon.

Hot wind blew my hair back from my face as I focused on my dragon sense. It tugged, strong and sure. I glanced at my companions and said, "Left."

We had no way of knowing where the Pool of Enchantment was located, but thought it might be away from the portal. Nix had said Dr. Garriso believed it was a safety precaution to have the portal entrance located farther from the pool to limit situations like this occurring. When he'd built the portal, the Monster had probably expected someone to fight back. Keeping the portal away from its battery made it harder for us to destroy it.

"I like the desert," Nix muttered. "At least we can see what's coming."

"And it's like being at the beach," Del said. "Except drier."

"Don't wish for the beach or we might get some water," I said, remembering our icy plunge the last time we were here.

A second later, the ground dropped out from under us. But instead of water, there was nothing. Cliffs rose steeply in front of me as I plummeted into an enormous gorge. I shrieked, my stomach caught in my throat, and I clawed at the air, somehow managing to catch onto a ledge. My fingers dragged at it, but I lost my grip and fell again.

On either side, Nix and Del plummeted, along with the Nullifier.

"Aidan!" I couldn't see him, but I prayed he'd turned into a griffin.

Except he couldn't carry all of us. My skin grew cold. My heart threatened to break my ribs.

He couldn't carry all of us.

There was only one way out of this. Could I even do it?

I squeezed my eyes shut and tried to focus, reaching out for Aidan's shifting power. I caught hold of his signature—the scent of the forest, the sound of crashing waves, the taste of chocolate. I drew on his magic, using my Mirror Mage skills to imitate his ability to shift.

"Griffin, griffin, griffin," I whispered.

I'd only ever tried to turn into land mammals before, but none of those would help me now. Turning into a griffin was a stretch, but since Aidan was hopefully already in his griffin form, it should be easier than doing it from scratch. Mirroring an animal that was near me was easier.

Wind whipped by as magic filled my being. Warmth flowed through my limbs.

Suddenly, the wind changed. Instead of blowing my hair and clothes, it ruffled my feathers and fur. I opened my eyes and could see great clawed feet in front of me. My wings flapped awkwardly in the wind.

I could fly!

Sort of.

Below, the ground was growing closer. I flapped my wings harder, trying to propel myself upward. They caught on the wind, pushing me toward the sky. I laughed, but it came out as a strange squawk. Then I whirled on the air and dived for the nearest body that had been falling alongside mine.

Nix. Her black hair whipped in the wind as she screamed. I plunged, swooping below her to catch her on my back.

Her weight forced me down. I beat my wings harder, struggling to keep us airborne.

One person was the maximum I could carry, and even now, we were half flying/half falling. My best efforts were just slowing our descent. No doubt I was a smaller, more awkward version of Aidan's griffin.

"Woo!" Nix's jubilant shout sounded from above. "Go, Cass!"

I beat my wings harder, my new muscles burning, determined to get us to safety and give a good showing as a griffin. If Aidan hadn't turned into one, too, I was going to need to find some more strength in the next two seconds in order to save him and Del and the Nullifier.

It would be an impossible task.

I spun on the breeze, searching for Aidan and the others, praying that he had caught them. My claws curled in fear as I sought him out.

The sight of Aidan as a griffin, Del and the Nullifier on his broad back, sent relief streaking through me. I gave a victorious cry, the noise coming out as a strange, birdlike shriek. Nix laughed.

I flew toward Aidan, the wind in my feathers. Lightness and joy surged through me, the most intense I'd ever felt. I'd saved us.

Together, we glided down onto the valley floor below. A wide river wound through the valley, tall pines on either side. With my enhanced griffin hearing, I could detect animals rustling in the underbrush by the river.

When I landed, I staggered a bit on my strange new legs, and Nix tumbled off my back. In a flash of gray light, Aidan turned back into himself. Nix dragged her phone from her pocket and snapped a picture of me right before I called upon my magic to shift back. I tried my best to focus on having clothes and my daggers when I turned back into a human.

Warmth filled my limbs, light flashed around me, and a second later, I swayed on my real legs. I was grateful to see that I was still wearing pants, though I had on only one boot and my leather jacket, but no shirt beneath.

At least I was decent. And my daggers had made it.

"That was amazing!" Nix cried.

"Thanks." I dragged a shaky hand through my hair.

The Nullifier sat heavily on a rock. "I am not used to all of this excitement."

I didn't want to mention that this might be the dullest part of our trip.

"Here." Nix handed me another boot and a t-shirt that she'd conjured.

"Thanks." I turned and dragged off my jacket, then pulled the t-shirt on. Aidan joined me as I sat on the ground and tugged on the boot.

He crouched next to me. "You did good. Changing in midair like that is pretty amazing."

I grinned up at him. "Thanks. Did I look good?"

"Umm…" Aidan's gaze was conflicted.

Del laughed.

"Well," Nix said. "You were a good flier. That's all that matters."

"Let me see the picture you took," I groused.

She grinned and handed over her phone. I glanced down at the image and cringed.

The sorriest looking griffin I'd ever seen stared back at me. Brown and mottled, with patchy fur and feathers, it was half the size of Aidan's griffin and looked like a fairytale reject.

"Whew," I said.

"You'll be a better-looking, stronger griffin with practice," Aidan said. "But for now, you changed in midair and saved your *deirfiúr's* life. That's all that counts."

"I think being an actual cool-looking griffin is your specialty," I said. And we didn't have time to worry about what an ugly griffin I made.

The scenery around us already wavered then changed to a new place. We were back in the desert. In the distance, a green oasis beckoned. My dragon sense tugged. The blue pool was so brilliant it made my eyes hurt, but it was the purple glow from within that made my heart gallop.

"There!" I pointed.

I ran, the sand dragging at my feet. My lungs burned from the hot air, but I pushed myself harder. We were still several hundred yards away, but it felt so close I could taste the cool water in the pool.

A moment later, the serene quiet of the desert was replaced with the cacophonous sounds of an exotic bazaar. I pulled to a halt, my friends behind me. Heat blazed down on the many stalls filled with goods of every imaginable type—food, wine, jewels, fabric, toys, dishes. Like a fantasy department store in the desert. Colorful awnings stretched as far as I could see, a maze of people and merchandise.

Languages I didn't recognize flew around us as shopkeepers shouted about their wares. Magic ricocheted on the air. Supernaturals populated this bazaar, not humans. There were even some demons, just like at the dance club from before.

"Does the Pool of Enchantment continue to move?" the Nullifier asked.

"No, I don't think so," I said. "But the scenery around it does. We just need to get to it. Once we're there, the pool itself should stay stable."

"Good." His wide gaze flitted everywhere, clearly nervous.

I nodded, then focused on my dragon sense, letting it pull me through the crowd. We went single file through the narrow passageways between stalls, dodging bodies and offerings of samples of sweets and fruits.

"What have we here?" a rumbling voice said from beside me.

I glanced around to see a huge form stepping out from between two stalls. His eerie silver eyes glinted.

Tracker demon. And there were two behind him.

My muscles tensed.

"A FireSoul wandering around the bazaar." His dark gaze darted behind me to Nix and Del. The Nullifier and Aidan took up the rear, but he didn't bother looking at them. "Three FireSouls."

"Our quota for the next three years," the demon behind him said.

I called upon my lightning, ready to blast him away. But his big arm flashed out and grabbed me before I could so much as let the lightning crackle inside of me.

A second later, I was standing inside a dark dungeon, the cold seeping through my jacket, into my heart.

Shit, shit, shit.

I was a dead girl.

"The boss will be pleased with you," the Tracker demon rumbled.

Hell no, that wasn't going to happen. I launched myself at him and swung my fist, aiming for his face. It collided with his nose, pain singing up my arm. He roared as blood sprayed. I heaved my knee between his legs, but he didn't crumble like I expected.

Instead, he backhanded me across the face so hard that I flew through the air and crashed into the wall. Pain flared in my head as it cracked against the stone.

Darkness followed.

CHAPTER THIRTEEN

Light flashed as the door to the cell opened. I scuttled back, pressing myself against the wall. On either side of me, another girl huddled, shrinking back from the figure who loomed in the door.

They were here for one of us.

Me?

My skin crawled, ice seeping through my veins, freezing me solid against the cold stone floor. They'd taken so many girls before. Would I be next?

I was only fifteen. I had barely lived. Was this to be my end?

The guard pointed one big finger and growled, "You."

Without a shadow of a doubt, he pointed at me. My heart stopped.

He stomped forward on huge feet and grabbed me by the arm. His iron grip crushed my muscles. The other girls clung to my hands, trying to hold me back as if they could save me.

Nothing could save me.

Girls left. If they came back at all, it was different. They were collared or worse.

That would be me now.

I thrashed, trying to break free of his grasp, as the guard dragged me from the room. The rough stone scraped my bare feet, but I dug in, trying to keep myself from being dragged into the hall. The cell was terrible, but it was familiar. In there, all I knew was hunger and dark and fear.

Out here, there were worse terrors.

The dim light in the hall was no easier on my eyes. I didn't remember how long I'd been in the dark, but it'd been a long time. The guard dragged me up a flight of wooden stairs, then out a door and into an ornate hallway with silk wallpaper and wood paneling. A fancy manor house, though I didn't remember it from my trip to the cell. I didn't remember how I had gotten to the cell at all.

I gabbed for an iron light fixture as the guard pulled me down the hall. My fingers brushed it for one short moment before I was yanked away.

"Quit struggling," the guard muttered.

I kicked him in the shin, but all it did was send pain singing up my leg. A second later, he tossed me into a room. There was a flash of bookshelves and plush furniture before I thudded to the ground and skidded on a gleaming wooden floor. I scrambled into a crouch as my skin grew cold, then glanced around wildly like a trapped animal.

"She's feisty," the guard said, his gaze directed over my head.

I spun, staying crouched low to the ground, hating that the motion was so familiar, so instinctual.

"Shackle her, then." The voice was so cold it shivered along my skin. It was even scarier than the words.

Footsteps thudded behind me. I lunged to the side, but I was too slow. The guard's big hand snagged my arm, his grip bruising. Cold metal clamped around one of my wrists, then the other, binding my arms behind me.

Terror surged, a fear so great that it felt like acid in my veins. It scrabbled through me with sharp claws as I cowered on the floor.

The guard lifted me by the arm, nearly dislocating my shoulder, and spun me to face the man with the cold voice.

He looked so normal—thin and brown-haired and boring—that the evil in his gaze stood out starkly. I cringed back, whimpering.

The man crooked his finger, gesturing the guard forward.

Despite my terror, instinct made me kick and thrash, determined not to go easily to my doom. But I was like a fly in a web.

The evil man's pale hand reached for me, gripping my thin dress and dragging me toward him. He was so close I could make out his pores and the muddy speckles in his irises. I yanked at my bonds, but all I did was scrape the skin from my wrists.

The pain was nothing though. Gray flame was starting to lick its way across the man's skin, the heat scorching. It flickered toward me, crawling up his arm to my chest. When it jumped onto the front of my dress, I screamed.

The flame felt like knives digging into my flesh. It rooted around inside of me, seeking out my power.

This man was a FireSoul, like me, I realized. Terror flared, greater than the pain of his gray fire. He was going to take my power! I'd never done that myself, but I knew what it was.

"No!" I cried. My power was my soul. It was me.

"So rare," the man muttered, his gaze alight with greed.

I thrashed, but pain and my bound hands made me weak. The flame was eating me from the inside, consuming me. My vision was fading.

The man's face twisted with frustration. Sweat dripped down his temples.

"Why isn't it working?" He shook me.

My head lolled on my neck as my vision narrowed to a pinprick of light. I was sure my ribs were being torn open, my heart and lungs plucked out by the beak of a hungry bird.

A spot of cool relief glowed on my chest.

My locket? Consciousness began to fade.

"Why isn't it working?" the evil man yelled.

Spit hit my face. The pain in my chest surged until I was certain that I was being consumed by the man's gray flame. My power was waning, struggling to stay inside of me.

But I was losing it. I could feel it being peeled away. Crushed. Immolated.

Gone.

I didn't know what was going on, but as my mind retreated inside of itself, I knew I was losing part of my soul.

Consciousness jerked me from the memory. I rolled onto my side and vomited, my chest heaving. When I was empty, I struggled to my knees and crawled toward the corner.

I shoved myself back into it, the cold bite of stone so familiar. I'd spent part of my childhood here. This was the cell Nix, Del, and I had fled.

But what had that nightmare just been? An event I'd suppressed? How had I not noticed the feeling of missing one of my powers? If it felt anything like the Nullifier suppressing my powers, it was terrible.

I shuddered at the memory of the horrible pain. It was no surprise I'd repressed it. The Monster had stolen my root power. Or destroyed it. I didn't think he'd taken it as his own, though. He'd been so angry. So frustrated. That meant he hadn't gotten ahold of it, right?

But it was also no longer my own. I couldn't even remember what it was. I was a FireSoul, but what else was I? When I'd learned that I'd stolen my Mirror Mage power, I'd thought perhaps my root power had been that I was a FireSoul. I didn't know if that was possible, but I'd assumed it. I'd never imagined I'd had a power stolen from me.

I'd been wrong.

I was some kind of Magica, but I didn't know what kind.

A blue light glowed from the other wall, catching my eye. Del? Hope flared in my chest.

A moment later, Del drifted through the wall in her phantom form, a ghostly blue apparition of her normal self. I leapt to my feet and raced to her.

"Del!" I whispered. "Where is Nix? Is the Monster here? I think this is his home."

She nodded, her blue face transparent. "It is. I remember this place. Nix is in a cell down the way. She's conjuring a key. I don't know if the Monster is here."

"A key? Is her power not blocked?" Most magical cells blocked the inhabitant's power.

"There's a block," Del whispered. "But it's only strong enough for children and low power mages. Nix is too powerful. It's taking her a while, but she thinks she'll have a key soon."

Anger bubbled like hot tar in my chest. So he preyed on kids. "Bastard. Are there any children here?"

"Not that I could find," Del said. "And I floated through all the cells on this floor. But some of them looked recently used. If there are children here, they might be elsewhere."

"Damn it." Did we have to choose between looking for missing children and saving Magic's Bend?

That was too terrible a choice.

A moment later, a scratching noise sounded at the door. A key in the lock. The heavy wooden door creaked open, and Nix crept in. Her face was pale in the gloom, reflecting slightly blue in the light of Del's phantom form.

"Are you okay?" she whispered.

"Good enough to run for it," I said. But okay? Not even close. "Lets do a quick sweep. See if we can find any kids."

Nix and Del nodded.

"I've checked this hall," Del said. "No guards, no kids. I think we're new additions. We've only been here ten minutes. Someone will probably be coming for us soon."

We snuck out into the hall. I glanced right, not surprised to see the big wooden door that I'd gone through twice in my nightmares. Once to have my powers destroyed, the second time to escape—though I hadn't remembered going through it the first time at that point. I must have repressed the memory.

Or had it stolen.

How many times had I been violated here?

I shook away the dark thought and glanced left. Another door, this one smaller.

"Have you checked through there?" I asked Del.

She shook her head, so I set off in that direction, keeping my footsteps light and my hand gripped on Righty, my favored dagger. I didn't want to use lightning here, not when thunder would follow it. The noise would alert any guards.

Quietly, I pushed open the door. A narrow set of stone steps led down, looking like they were leading to the basement of a haunted castle.

Even farther underground? The Monster had a creepy underground mole's labyrinth. But if there were any more prisoners, they would probably be down there.

Slowly, we crept down the stairs, our way lit by the glow of Del's phantom form. The door at the bottom of the stairs had no lock. After listening for a moment, I sucked in a deep breath and pushed it open.

A wave of malevolence rolled out of the dimly lit room, making my skin feel sticky. Candles perched on tables and shelves, illuminating a large space that was lavishly furnished. A stooped figure sat in a plush armchair in the middle of the room.

The malevolence rolled off of him. If he were a prisoner, which I wasn't entirely certain of given the lavishness of his quarters and the lack of a lock on the door, he deserved it.

"Who is there?" His voice creaked with age.

"Mr. Orriordor sent us," I improvised.

"He did not!" The old man's milky gaze snapped to my own. "You!"

"Me?"

"I recognize you."

"A seer," Del whispered from beside me.

I hurried to his side. The stench of malevolence was worse near him. Dark magic. No doubt he helped the Monster commit his evil deeds.

"What do you know about me?" I demanded.

"Payment first."

I almost growled as I thrust out my dagger and held it at his neck. His hand gripped my wrist, and I shuddered at the feel of his cold skin. Evil seemed to seep through into my flesh as the chill soaked into my muscles and up my arm.

"How's this for payment?" I demanded and I pressed the knife against his skin. "Tell me what I want to know, and I won't slit your throat."

His lips peeled back from his teeth, revealing crooked yellow fangs. I pressed the blade harder until blood welled. His muddy eyes rolled back in his head until only the whites showed.

Was that how he had his visions?

"What do you know about me?" I demanded.

"The gifted."

"What?"

"The gifted."

Frustration welled. "Anything more?"

"The gifted."

Damn it. "What about my *deirfiúr*?"

"The gifted."

Was he just repeating himself? "What does Orriordor want?"

"Power." His white eyes rolled in their sockets.

"From who?"

"Everyone."

"To do what with?"

"Destroy them."

My muscles tightened. Frustration beat in my chest, a living thing threatening to consume me. I met Del and Nix's gazes and saw the same feeling reflected in their eyes. Destroying people was such a broad, generic villain's goal.

It was also pretty much the height of evil. And after my nightmares, I wasn't going to underestimate the Monster.

"Destroy who?" I bit off the words.

"All of them."

"The children?"

The seer shook his head. "They are fuel. Soldiers. Destroy the powerful."

That was a lot of people.

"Who are the powerful?"

"Destroy them!" His voice boomed in the dark room.

I shook him, wanting any kind of clear answer. But seers weren't known for their clear answers.

"Stop!" Del hissed. "That's all he knows. We don't want him to alert the guards."

"He's probably the seer who scried for us!" I said. "And who helps the Monster find the other FireSouls. Who gives the Tracking demons their leads."

Del's gaze darkened as she looked at the seer. "Do you scry for FireSouls?"

He nodded, his eyes still whited out.

"Are there any child prisoners here?"

"Not at present." He licked his lips, and my stomach churned.

"But another time?"

He shrugged. "It is likely. They are often here before they learn."

"Learn what?"

"Learn. Learn, learn, learn." He muttered until I shook him. I was losing him. Seers were often not of their right mind, and I didn't think this one had started out sane.

"Have you told us all you know?" I pressed the blade deeper into his neck. Not enough to kill, but to encourage.

"For now," he said.

We didn't have time to wait around and see if he had any more visions. I withdrew my knife and turned to my *deirfiúr*.

"We should go," I said.

"Should we kill him?" Del asked.

I glanced at him, both repulsed by the evil I could feel rolling off him and hesitant to kill someone so physically frail. I hadn't had a chance to make up my mind when a blur of silver flashed through the air.

A dagger sank into his right eye, killing him almost instantly. There was a brief second where my FireSoul flared, desperate to jump on him and steal his power. I shoved it back, and he died so quickly that I didn't have a chance to act on the urge, even if I had wanted to.

My gaze flew to my *deirfiúr*. Nix lowered her hand.

"You've had to do a lot of the hard stuff lately," she said. "It was my turn. He couldn't be left alive to scry for more of our kind."

There would be more seers where he came from, but she was right. He was nothing but evil and had no doubt contributed to many deaths.

"Thanks. Now let's get the hell out of here and close the portal."

"Do you have enough juice to teleport us?" Nix asked Del.

Del shook her head. "I don't want to risk it if I don't have to. I'm running low as it is, and I want to make sure I get us out of here when the portal closes."

"Then we try to sneak out," I said. "Find Aidan and the Nullifier and get this done."

We left the room and crept back up the stairs to the main dungeon. I shuddered as we made our way down the hall, now remembering the time I'd been dragged from the cell. I'd thought I'd escaped the Monster's wrath when he'd first held me prisoner.

I'd just forgotten.

We paused at the great wooden door at the end of the hall.

I turned to Nix and Del. "We sneak out. Let's not fight if we don't have to. I don't want to alert any more demons to the fact that we're here."

"And those Tracker demons probably went to fetch the Monster," Del said. "So let's hurry our butts outta here before he shows."

I nodded, then led the way up the stairs, a horrible sense of deja vu stalking me. I couldn't escape this hell hole soon enough. Maybe this place held more secrets about what had happened to me, but I wasn't going to stick around to find out.

We reached the top of the stairs. Experimentally, I tried using my new Illusion power to turn myself invisible.

"Whoa," Del whispered. "Good work. But I can still see your head."

Damn. It'd have to do. I'd be sure to practice my new skill more if we made it out of here.

Slowly, I pushed open the door at the top of the stairs and peered out. A smoke demon stood a few feet down the hall. His head whipped toward me, his black gaze meeting mine. His eyes widened.

Shit.

I flung Righty through the crack in the door, then yanked Lefty out of its thigh sheath. As the demon collapsed, I pricked my fingertip with Lefty. My blood ignited the spell that called Righty back. It pulled itself out of the demon's chest and flew through the air toward me. I snagged it. I might not have used my daggers in a while, but it was like riding a bicycle. A pointy, sharp-as-hell bicycle.

But where there was one smoke demon, there was usually more.

"We've got trouble," I whispered back to Nix and Del as I pushed my way out into the hall.

Four smoke demons waited. One muttered into a comms charm that was similar to the one hanging around my neck.

"Fight fast," I said. "Reinforcements are coming."

Del drew her sword and swung it in a graceful arc as she stepped forward. She dodged a blast of burning smoke and swiped out with her blade, removing the hand of the demon who'd threatened her.

I called on my Mirror Mage powers, reaching out for the demon's magic. Time to fight fire with fire. Or smoke with smoke, in this case. The smoky bite of the demon's magic filled my nose as I gathered up the blazing cloud and threw a blast at the demon nearest me.

The heat singed my fingertips as it left and bowled him over. Nix leapt upon him, her fist gripped around a long dagger that she'd conjured. Quickly, she slit his throat.

Del finished off her demon by plunging her blade into his heart while I threw another blast of smoke at the biggest demon in the bunch. Nix finalized the job with her blade.

Del and I tag-teamed the final demon, satisfaction lancing through me as she plunged her blade deep into his heart. We were a good team.

A shout sounded behind us. I glanced back.

Shit.

Six demons charged down the hall.

"Run!" I yelled.

We sprinted down the hall, jumping over the bodies of the demons we'd felled. I passed the room where I'd had my power obliterated and just barely repressed the urge to vomit. We skidded out into the foyer and sprinted for the door, an eerie reproduction of our first race to freedom.

I threw myself at the door, shoving it open and bursting out into the heat of the desert. We clambered down the stairs, our feet sinking into the hot sand as we raced for freedom. I wished Aidan were here so that I could mirror his griffin power. I might turn into an ugly beast, but I was so freaked out right now I knew I could definitely fly both my *deirfiúr* to freedom.

No luck, though.

The demons burst through the door behind us as the scenery began to waver.

Please put us back in that dance club.

I could definitely lose these guys in there.

Instead, we got my worst nightmare.

Lava stretched out in front of us, a seething ocean of neon orange death.

"Shit!" Nix screamed.

Magma rolled toward us, an oncoming wave of heat and molten rock.

"Go back!" I spun on my heels, Del and Nix at my side, and ran back toward the smoke demons.

Screw stealth.

I called upon my lightning, letting it crackle and burn beneath my skin as I built up a big enough bolt. At my side, Nix conjured a bow and arrow and fired into the crowd of shadow demons. She liked weapons as much as I did, so her aim was good. Three demons fell in quick succession.

I sent a massive bolt of lightning at the two demons nearest me. Thunder cracked as the bolt struck, and the demons collapsed.

Del raced ahead, safe in her phantom form. When she reached the last remaining demon, she turned corporeal long enough to take off his head with a flying leap and sweep of her sword.

She landed and turned to us, panting. "We cannot get a freaking break."

I glanced at the lava that flowed toward us, then back at the Monster's mansion. More enemies would come from it soon if we didn't get out of here. The Trackers still hadn't shown up with the Monster, but they would.

The air didn't waver. No change of scenery was coming.

"I think we gotta risk it, Del," I said. "The waypoint is weird, right? So it's not as far a distance as out in the real world."

"Yeah." Her gaze clouded with doubt. "But I don't know if I'll be able to get us all back when the portal closes."

Indecision warred within me. I could feel the heat of the lava at my back and the glower of the Monster's mansion ahead of me. But it was the sight of him striding out the door and down the stone steps that made up my mind. Now that I realized how many powers he'd likely stolen, he seemed invincible.

"Risk it!" I sprinted to Del. "Monster incoming!"

CHAPTER FOURTEEN

A second later, we arrived back at the bazaar where we'd first been snatched. Sound and color were a wild cacophony around us as the heat of the desert and hundreds of bodies pressed in on us. A woman dressed in colorful scarves shrieked about fish for sale and a man who looked just like Aladdin—the cartoon one— shouted over her, trying to sell CD players.

"Fates, I hope that didn't screw us," Del said. "I really don't know if I'll be able to get us all back."

"We'll worry about that when the time comes." A man jostled into me and I shoved him away.

"Wench!" he spat, then disappeared through the bustling crowd.

We needed to get the hell out of this bazaar. I focused on my dragon sense to find Aidan and the Nullifier. The familiar tug pulled at my middle.

"Come on!" I called. We raced through the stalls, not stopping to say "excuse me" or even "move your ass."

We just bowled people over and shoved by them as we ran. Trackers and shadow demons could be anywhere. Because even though the waypoint was everywhere at once, it was the Monster's world more than it was ours. He and his minions knew it better than we ever would.

I caught sight of Aidan's dark hair, an easy feat considering he stood a head taller than everyone else.

"Aidan!"

He turned immediately, relief in his gray gaze. I reached him before he could take a step and threw myself into his arms. He hugged me tight, his strong arms banishing the last of my fear over my nightmare. It would come back in the dark, but for now, I was strong.

I pushed away from him. "We've got to go!"

He nodded. I glanced to his left to see the Nullifier, his gaze tired and stressed, then focused on my dragon sense and the portal we sought.

"This way!" I grabbed Aidan's hand.

I set off through the crowd again, glancing behind to make sure the others followed. Del and Nix bracketed the Nullifier, protecting him as we pushed through the crowd. We'd nearly reached the edge of the bazaar when our surroundings wavered, the air shimmering. I held my breath and prayed for something favorable.

Yellow sand stretched out before us, waving hills like an ocean.

More freaking desert. Same oppressive heat, but instead of a crowd jostling us from all sides, sand sucked at our feet.

But an oasis glimmered ahead. The lack of obstacles in our path meant I could actually see the end goal instead of just feel it. It spurred me on.

"There!" I pointed.

I ran, but I was so slow. The sand dragged at me, holding me back. Aidan was faster than me, but not by much.

"Aidan! Fly the Nullifier to the pool. We'll follow."

"I'll take you as well," he said.

"No. You'll be faster alone. He's the one who needs to get there."

"But we all need to get out," Aidan said. "When the portal closes, we won't have long to escape."

I didn't tell him that my *deirfiúr* and I weren't sure we *would* all get out, but he was right. We needed to stick together.

"Fine. Take Del and the Nullifier. I'll shift too and take Nix."

Aidan nodded.

I reached out for his power, grasping onto the evergreen scent and crashing wave sound, searching out his ability to shift. I let the magic fill my limbs, warming me from the inside. My bones twisted and changed, a process that was thankfully painless, and a second later I stood taller, my clawed feet digging into the sand.

I knelt on one knee so that Nix could scramble onto my back.

"Looking better!" she called.

I grinned—or thought I did, if beaks could grin— and pushed off the ground, my strong wings carrying me into the sky. It was awkward at first, but I caught on quicker this time and flew after Aidan.

Nix shrieked, her joy obvious. My joy was palpable, too, singing through me. I loved my power now that I'd embraced it. It gave me so many gifts. Completed me.

Whatever I'd lost when I was younger, at least I had this. I was too strong now for the Monster to steal it from me.

The scenery around us changed as we flew, turning to ancient forest. Scraggly oaks reached up from the ground, their claw-like branches grasping for us. Shade cast the forest floor in shadow. The woods looked like the type dark faeries would gather within.

I could still see the pool from my lofty vantage point, though it had changed slightly. The water still glimmered blue with the portal's purple sheen, but the land surrounding it was now made of great boulders dotted with ferns and moss. An enchanted glen.

I pushed myself harder, beating my wings with everything I had. I was a griffin—mostly—and I could fly, but not like Aidan. He was strength and grace in animal form when he flew. His strong wings left me in the dust.

I squinted against the wind and raced to keep up.

Suddenly, a massive fireball flew from the ground, straight for Aidan. He dodged, wheeling on the wind, his golden wings glinting in the light. Another blazing orange fireball followed. He dodged again, Del and the Nullifier clinging to his back.

The third and fourth fireballs got him, shooting from the trees below and hitting him square in the underbelly, one after the other. He flailed as his wings failed, then he plummeted.

I shrieked and dived low to follow. More fireballs shot from the trees. A defense line we'd triggered? Guards? I'd seen no guards while the desert had been here, but we'd been farther away then. They could have been hiding amongst the palms and ferns.

"Fireball to the right!" Nix yelled.

I dodged the flame as best I could, escaping two fireballs that singed me with heat as they passed. My wings ached as I struggled to maneuver.

"Fireball left!" Nix screamed.

I shot right, but an enormous oak was in my way. I jerked back, narrowly avoiding the trunk, but pain blazed in my wing and the smell of burning feathers hit my nose.

I'd been hit!

I struggled to keep beating my wings, but they faltered, the injured one barely moving. With one wing, I couldn't stay aloft. I fell, flapping my good wing in an attempt to control my landing. Nix clung to my back.

"The clearing to the left!" Nix screamed.

I aimed for it, flailing as we plummeted. I kept my footing as I landed, galloping across the ground on wild legs I no longer controlled. Unable to stay upright any longer, I skidded on my knees in the dirt, flinging Nix off my back. She flew head over ass, crashed, then slid on the dirt.

I struggled to my feet, wincing at the pain in my left leg, then called upon my magic. It flowed through me, warm and comforting, turning me back into my human form. Nix scrambled upright, her hair covering her face, then ran to me.

"You okay?" Nix's gaze was wild as it skimmed over my form.

"Fine." I was even wearing all of my clothes this time. "Let's go!"

We sprinted through the forest but kept low to the ground.

Where was Aidan?

It was darker than it should have been in the shelter of the gnarled oaks, as if some kind of black magic protected this place, and it made it hard to see. Colored lights glittered amongst the trees. Dark faeries, the tiny apparitions that wreaked havoc with travelers. An ancient tower loomed in the distance, evil radiating from its gray stones.

The sounds of a battle drew us to Aidan and Del, who fought demons only fifty yards from the pool. Over a dozen smoke demons bombarded them, their clouds of burning smoke flying through the air. The Nullifier huddled against a tree and cast a protective circle of anti-magic around himself.

I threw myself into the fray, gathering up my lightning and blasting the nearest demon. Thunder cracked as he crashed to the ground, his gray form alight with electricity.

Aidan stood at the base of a giant oak, hurling jets of flame at any demon who approached. He lit up three in the short time I watched.

Del danced amongst the horde in her phantom form, immune to their smoke. She went corporeal long enough to slice limbs and lop off heads. Nix jumped in with her to conjure grenades that she hurled at the outlying demons.

"To your left!" I screamed at Nix.

A demon had snuck up behind her. His blast of smoke got her in the arm, but she ducked and pivoted, conjuring a sword that she swung one-armed with deadly accuracy. The demon's head tumbled to the ground. She clutched her injured arm and glanced around for more demons to fight.

There were only two left before the way was clear and I could get the Nullifier to the pool. The water glittered beckoningly.

I raced to the Nullifier, jumping over boulders and dodging trees to get to him.

We were so close. Almost there.

The air shimmered. Dark magic shook the air.

I stumbled, recognizing the signature.

The scent of rot and decay filled my nose just before the Monster appeared, a Tracker demon at his side. My heart froze as I skidded to a halt, my gaze glued to the Monster. His pressed suit looked so out of place in the forest, but his hulking demon sidekick fit right in. The Tracker demon surged toward my friends, but the Monster turned his gaze on the Nullifier, who was still over a dozen yards from me.

I called upon my lightning, building the biggest bolt I'd ever created. It crackled and burned in my chest, ready to fly. But before I could send it, the Monster threw a sonic boom at the Nullifier. The ricochet alone knocked me on my ass. I skidded in the dirt, then scrambled up to see the Monster throw another boom.

This one hit the Nullifier dead on and threw him against the tree behind him. The first must have broken down his no-magic shield, but the second…

He didn't move.

No!

I threw my bolt of lightning at the Monster, taking advantage of his distraction with the Nullifier. Thunder cracked as it hit him, vibrating my bones. He convulsed and fell; my heart soared. Victory tasted sweet, though it wouldn't last. He'd rise soon. I wouldn't stay to watch.

I sprinted for the Nullifier, yelling, "Cover me!"

My friends had polished off the demons and turned their attention to the Monster, who had climbed to his feet. As I ran, Nix lobbed grenades—which were a bitch to dodge even if you were a supernatural—while Aidan threw enormous blasts of flame that exploded against the Monster's shield. Aidan shifted tactics, calling upon his Elemental Mage power to disrupt the earth beneath the Monster's feet. It rose as a craggy hill, throwing the Monster to his back.

His gaze caught mine as he fell. Fire blazed in his eyes. He stretched his hand out toward me, but nothing happened. I grinned and sprinted harder. I was only a few yards from the Nullifier now.

Something hard snapped around my waist, a massive arm that jerked me up into the air. I thrashed and kicked my legs, clawing at whatever had grabbed me. Rough bark bit into my fingertips. I looked down. A tree branch had grabbed me, yanking me high into the air and holding me like King Kong had held Whats-her-name.

The Monster could control the forest?

We were screwed.

I pulled my obsidian blade from its sheath and hacked at the branch as I watched Del race toward the

Monster, her invincible blue form transparent in the dim light. Fear chilled my skin as she charged. She ran straight through his barrier, her phantom form not stopped by his magic, but when she went corporeal to strike, he was faster. Before her sword blow could land, he'd thrown a sonic boom at her that sent her hurtling backward. She crashed into a tree, then collapsed.

I screamed, hacking at the tree limb, but it did no good. My blade was nothing against the enchanted wood.

Del wasn't rising.

"Help!" I screamed. I didn't know who I was calling to—all my backup was here and totally occupied. But Del wasn't getting up and fear for her made me crazy.

A flash of orange light caught my eye, then blue. I jerked my head left.

The four dragonets fluttered nearby—fire, water, smoke, and stone—and all looked at me, their gazes expectant.

What the hell? Had I called them? Who cared.

I pointed to Del. "Help her!"

The sparkling blue water dragonet zoomed off, heading straight for Del. The fire dragonet flew behind me, its warmth grazing my cheek as it passed. I craned my neck to look. The dragonet wrapped its body around the tree limb, its nose touching its tail. Smoke rose from the limb as the wood burned away.

Wood creaked and groaned, then snapped. I plummeted. Something hard pushed at my butt and fluttered against my sides. I glanced down. The stone dragonet was trying to break my fall, but it was far too small.

It slowed my descent, at least, flying away at the last second so that I wouldn't crush it. I crashed to the ground, then scrambled to my feet. Del was rising as well, her hair wet from the water dragonet.

She charged the Monster, who was still holding my friends off. Nix was down, but struggling to her feet.

"Help them!" I cried at the dragonets.

They surged into the fray, flame and water, smoke and stone.

I ran to the Nullifier and I fell to my knees at his side. His face was pale, his mouth slack. My skin chilled.

I shook his frail shoulder. "Wake up!"

His eyelids fluttered, revealing slivers of his eyes.

"Come on! You have to be okay," I said.

"I'm…not." He coughed through the words. Blood appeared at the corner of his mouth. "Trauma can…kill me. This is that trauma."

Tears rolled down my face, tears over the loss of Magic's Bend and the guilt that I'd dragged this man into this. To his death.

"You must take my power," he said, then gasped. "Finish the job."

I stumbled back. Take his power? It would crush my own. Turn me powerless. I'd just started to embrace it. I liked my power. I *loved* it. And even when I hadn't been using it, it'd still been part of me. Taking his power would be like cutting out part of my soul. After all I'd lost, I'd lose the rest of my magic too?

It made me feel empty inside just to think of it.

The Nullifier was dying, his power there for the taking, but of course my FireSoul covetousness hadn't surged. My FireSoul didn't want anything to do with the Nullifier. He was anti-magic.

If we didn't kill the Monster here today, which I doubted we had the power to, I would still be hunted by him. Now powerless to protect myself.

"No," I said. "No, I can't. You're going to be okay. I'll take you to the pool, then Aidan will heal you."

He shook his head, his gaze sad, but I ignored it.

"Aidan!" I didn't worry about alerting the Monster to my plans. He knew our goal. "To the pool!"

I tried to ignore the pallor on the Nullifier's face as I focused on mirroring Aidan's shifter powers. I couldn't carry the Nullifier in my current form. Warmth filled my limbs as I envisioned the biggest, strongest griffin I could imagine. Magic sparked as I transformed.

My new, clawed feet were enormous. Twice as big as my old griffin form, though they still looked a bit odd. I turned toward the Nullifier and scooped him up in my claws, gently as I could. As I launched myself into the air, I prayed that my friends could cover me.

I'd only beaten my wings a couple times when the odd sensation hit me. It felt off. Weak.

Death?

I glanced down at the Nullifier. He hung limply in the cradle of my claws, his eyes barely open. My heart thundered, fear tightening my throat. My enhanced griffin senses were picking up the Nullifier's looming death. The weakness of his breathing, the chill of his skin. His magic leaving him.

Frantically, I flapped my wings and ignored the pain of flying with my injured body, trying to reach the pool as quickly as possible. Aidan waited for us at the edge. I landed as gently as possible, laying the Nullifier on the soft moss.

I transformed back to human, stumbling on shaky legs, and begged, "Heal him!"

Aidan dropped to his knees by the Nullifier. Tears burned my eyes as I watched him gently place his big palms on the Nullifier's shoulders. The Nullifiers head lolled as he turned to look at me.

The tears spilled over my lids and onto my cheeks.

"I can't," Aidan said.

"I'm too far gone," the Nullifier croaked.

Aidan's eyes met mine. "I'm sorry, Cass. There's nothing I can do. The sonic boom created too much internal damage."

My gaze darted to the Nullifier.

"Do it," he breathed. "Or Victor Orriordor will win."

I glanced over my shoulder. Nix was down in the dirt, struggling to get up. Del was holding off the Monster, but barely. He'd ignited a line of blue flame behind her and Nix, trapping them against his sonic boom attacks. The dragonets were trying, zooming around the Monster, but they couldn't do much against him.

My friends couldn't hold out much longer. Magic's Bend couldn't hold out much longer. The whole city would be destroyed, homes demolished, lives lost.

I turned back to the Nullifier, my heart tearing in two. The pain nearly stole my breath.

"Go help them," I said to Aidan.

"Cass. Don't."

My gaze met his, briefly. He knew what this would do to me. I could see it in his eyes.

"Go," I said, pointing to my friends. "They need you."

He nodded once, his gaze resigned, but fiercely proud, then left.

Proud of me?

I pushed the thought aside as I fell to my knees at the Nullifier's side. He looked so frail. A shadow of his former self, which hadn't been substantial to begin with.

"Thank you for trying," I said as I pressed my hands to his shoulders. "I'm sorry I brought you to this."

"It is all right." His gaze was calm. Accepting. "I am four hundred and seventeen. I have lived a long life. It is time I did something good with it."

It didn't make it feel any better. Especially now that I remembered how it felt to have your powers stolen. Like flaming knives digging into your chest.

"Give my best to Aethelred." He coughed, blood marring his lips.

"Thank you again," I said, wanting to thank him a thousand times for what he'd done for us.

He nodded. "Do it."

Bile rose in my throat as I let my FireSoul power rise within me. White flame flickered along my skin, but it didn't reach out eagerly for the Nullifier as it normally would. I had to force it forward, had to make myself take his power. What I was doing wasn't natural. No supernatural in her right mind would give up her power like this.

But I had to do it.

The Nullifier gasped as the flame crawled over his chest. Sickness surged through me, turning my stomach, as I forced myself to complete this ugly deed. When his magic flowed into me, heaviness pulled at my limbs. Darkness rolled over my soul as the Nullifier's magic suppressed my own, an inky tar that I could imagine coating my organs.

The Nullifier's face turned gray as he gasped his last breath. I tumbled away from him, a horrible emptiness devouring my insides. Loss overwhelmed me, an emptiness that threatened to swallow me alive until I was nothing but a shell curled up on the ground.

It took all I had to stagger to my feet. The battle raged on as I stumbled toward the pool. The scent of the ocean wafted from the water, though it was just a small spring. The pool's magic must smell of the sea, perhaps even drawing power from that enormous natural force.

I had no idea what to do—how did the Nullifier use his magic?

I followed instinct, stepping into the cool water. Pebbles shifted beneath my boots as I waded deeper. Shivers wracked me, clinking my teeth together, partially from the cold and partially from the horror of what I'd just done.

When the water was up to my chest, I took a deep breath and submerged. The water glittered blue when I opened my eyes. I turned until I saw the faint glow of purple deep below me, then swam toward it, kicking hard.

Magic pulsed as I neared it, vibrating deep in my muscles. Awkwardly, I called upon the Nullifier's magic—the only magic I had left in my arsenal now that his had destroyed mine—and released it into the pond.

Gray light shined from me, drowning out the glittering blue and purple. The vibrations slowed as the Nullifier's magic—I couldn't think of it as my own—destroyed the spell powering the Pool of Enchantment.

My lungs burned as I used up my air, but I didn't surface. I couldn't be sure that I'd fully destroyed the portal, and there was no way in hell I was going to fail at this. Besides, I wasn't sure I even had the strength to swim for the surface. So I floated there, forcing the new power into the water.

When blackness sparkled at the edge of my vision, something hard jerked me from behind. Water flowed around me as I struggled. When I broke the surface, I gasped, my vision still fuzzy.

A slender arm wrapped around my middle and began to tow me to shore. The floral aroma of Nix's magic mixed with the scent of the portal's dying magic. What had once smelled like the ocean now had an overwhelming odor of dead fish. When I blinked the water from my eyes, the air around me shimmered grayish purple.

It was working. My magic was destroying the portal. I kicked to help Nix, glancing over my shoulder to see Del and Aidan still holding off the Monster. The dragonets launched their own attack at the monster, crashing against his shields.

Nix and I climbed out of the water and scrambled over the pebbly shore. Helplessness overwhelmed me as I ran for Del, unable to call upon lightning or fire or even my Shifter form. There was nothing but emptiness when I called for my magic.

Nix guarded me as we ran. I tried to produce the protective no-magic barrier, but I was tapped out. Or unskilled. It took all I had to suppress my nullification powers enough not to squash my friends' power. And I wasn't sure if I even accomplished that.

Pain exploded in my every bone. A force threw me across the clearing and I crashed to the ground. One of the Monster's sonic booms must have hit me.

Through bleary eyes, I saw my friends racing for me. All three limped, blood pouring from various wounds. They dived toward me, narrowly avoiding another sonic boom as dirt flew into the air from the force of the missed hit.

The Monster's roar of rage echoed through the woods as Del transported us out of the clearing. The Nullifier's body was the last thing I saw. Left behind.

Guilt streaked through me, gnawing at my insides.

We appeared at the portal in the desert a second later. It was far smaller than it had been, the glowing purple now faded lavender. My friends dragged me through it. I fell to my knees on the other side, the marble floor of the museum room biting into my bones.

But if we were here, in the museum, it meant it had worked, right?

The guards and the investigator who'd previously been frozen were sitting up from the floor, their eyes dazed. The dragonets were nowhere to be seen, no doubt disappearing the same way they'd appeared.

"Can you get us out of here?" I said between gasps to Del, who struggled to her knees beside me.

She nodded. "Out of the room, at least."

"Leave me. I'll deal with them," Aidan said.

"Thanks." I didn't want to be near the investigators right now. I needed to get myself together. And my *deirfiúr* were still FireSouls. They shouldn't be around them at all.

Del grabbed my hand and Nix's and squeezed tight.

"Take us to Aidan's," I said. I had no idea if I could control my nullifying powers enough not to quash our concealment charms, so Aidan's place was safest.

"On it," Del said.

We only made it as far as the parking lot across the street from the museum. The museum was no longer purple and the building looked almost normal. No more missing wings. On the lawn, Mordaca staggered to her feet, Aerdeca helping her.

"Tapped out," Del said. "We're lucky we all made it this far."

"Because we didn't have to take the Nullifier." I shivered with guilt.

Del had said she probably wouldn't have been able to get us all out of there. She hadn't even had to try.

CHAPTER FIFTEEN

Staying glued to the news coverage of families returning to Magic's Bend was the only way I kept from crying. I'd been holed up in Aidan's mansion since my *deirfiúr* and I had come here from the museum. As soon as I'd arrived yesterday morning, I'd commandeered the guest bedroom and I hadn't left.

We'd all slept for a solid twelve hours after receiving some medical care. Nix had had several broken bones and Del had had internal bleeding and a concussion from her collision with the tree, but they were largely better now. Aidan had escaped without major injury, primarily because his body was unusually tough, being the Origin and all.

My laundry list of injuries had healed with some magical help. Now, I was just moping. Nix and Del had kept me fueled with cheeseburgers and ice cream, but I could tell they were starting to lose patience.

But I didn't know how to function with half of myself gone. I almost wished my memory had been wiped like it had when the Monster had destroyed my root power. Or had he stolen it?

I really couldn't tell, and I hated that. If I couldn't remember what I'd lost, maybe I wouldn't be so damned depressed.

A loud knock sounded at the door.

"Open up!" Del shouted.

"Or we're breaking it down!" Nix yelled.

I flopped back onto the bed and stared at the ceiling. "It's open."

The door swung in and Del and Nix entered, each carrying a six-pack of PBR. The silver cans gleamed in the low light of the bedside lamp. I had the blinds drawn so that slivers of golden light striped across the floor.

I eyed the cans with a fraction of my usual interest. "Isn't it only eleven in the morning?"

Del shrugged. "It tastes like shit at any time of day, so why not drink it now?"

I tried to scowl at the insult to my beloved PBR, but couldn't manage much more than a grimace.

Nix flopped on the bed next to me and handed me a beer. I dragged myself upright until I leaned against the headboard and stared at her stonily.

"Drink it," she said. "If I have to, you have to."

"Why are you drinking it? You hate it."

"It's a show of solidarity, dumbass." She cracked the can open and took a sip, her forehead wrinkling. "We're going to drink one of these things you love so much and talk about all the good things we've got going on."

"Yeah. Can't be bummed when you're busy being grateful," Nix said.

"Good things? My chest feels like someone tore my heart out. I'm immortal, for magic's sake. That's awful.

233

Who wants to hang around forever after all their friends are dead?"

Nix grimaced, her eyes softening. "I know. I'm sorry. What you did was amazing."

Del reached for my hand and gave it a squeeze.

"Ugh, screw amazing. Who cares?" I'd do it again in a heartbeat—the news coverage I'd been watching kept reminding me of that—but it didn't matter that it was amazing or self-sacrificing or any of that bullshit. That stuff didn't bring back a person's powers. *Why* I'd done it didn't matter, only that I had.

And now that I had, I had to live with the aftermath. I was willing to, but I wasn't up for doing it gracefully yet.

"On the plus side, we're all alive." Del's gaze turned grim. "Except the poor Nullifier."

I lowered my beer, guilt resting heavily on my chest.

"He died a hero, at least," Nix said. "I heard that the Order of the Magica will hold a ceremony for him."

"That's good, he deserves it," I said. "And he seemed mostly at peace in the end."

He'd reminded me of Aaron, the first Magica whose power I'd stolen. Aaron had been ready to die as well. Why was it that so many people I encountered recently were happy to die? What kind of shitty world was I getting myself into?

Even with my powers gone and my soul pulverized, I didn't want to die. I wanted to mope and eat ice cream in the dark, but I didn't want to die.

"And you have cool dragon friends," Nix said. "What were those all about?"

"They're dragonets," I said. "They'd been the Nullifier's friends."

"Now they're your friends," Del said. "Dragon friends are definitely something to be grateful for."

"Yeah, you have a point." I glanced down at my beer. "I guess they've gone back to Switzerland."

"But you'll see them again," Nix said.

"I hope so."

"One thing to think about," Del said. "After giving up all your power so willingly, you can't exactly keep worrying you're a power hungry FireSoul, can you?"

"No. You're right about that." I knew the covetousness would come whenever I had an opportunity to steal a power, but I now knew I could definitely control it. I might enjoy taking powers, which was something I didn't actually like about myself, but I could deal with that too. As long as I was in control when I did it, and didn't take from an innocent, I could live with myself.

"So that's several things to be happy about," Nix said. "We're alive, we've saved Magic's Bend, we now have dragons for friends, and the Monster is at the waypoint and not on Earth."

"But he can get out," I said.

"Sure. But he can't find us still, not as long as you keep repressing your Nullification powers."

I nodded. It'd become second nature to me now, keeping the nullification locked up so it didn't screw with my concealment charm. That was one thing to be grateful for. I'd need more practice to be able to create a no-magic barrier, but at least I could be near my sisters.

"We just have to not run into him, and we'll be fine," Del said.

"Except we've been doing that a lot lately," Nix said. "He's everywhere we turn."

"We're going to have to find him," I said. "We can't keep running. He's going to find us. Those Tracker demons might not have been hunting for us specifically, but they know there are FireSouls in Magic's Bend. It's only a matter of time."

"Agreed," Del said. "We may have killed that seer, but he'll find another."

Nix nodded.

"Do you think he wanted the chalice?" Nix said.

"Maybe," Del said. "Or something else in the museum."

"Damn. I wish we'd figured it out."

"There hadn't exactly been time," Del said.

No, there hadn't. It'd taken everything we had to complete the goal and get out of there alive.

"I had another nightmare," I said. I'd meant to tell them sooner, but I'd been sleeping so much of the past twenty-four hours that I hadn't had a chance. I also hadn't wanted to talk about it. If I was going to open my mouth, it was going to be to shove a cheeseburger inside it.

Their gazes met mine.

Since my moping time had passed, I told them about the Monster stealing or destroying my root power and how I'd apparently repressed the trauma.

"You were too young to cope with it," Nix said.

"And you don't remember what your power was?" Del asked.

"No. Just like I don't remember anything before we were fifteen. I've no idea what it was." The memory of the locket cooling on my chest flashed in my mind. I raised my fingers to it. "But the locket felt strange as he was stealing my power."

"That's a clue," Del said. "Obviously."

"Obviously?"

"Yeah," Del said. "Aidan told me how Aethelred said to come back to him for more information about the locket. Aidan's had a guy camped out on Aethelred's doorstep for the last day, waiting for the old guy to return so that he can bring him to you."

Tears smarted my eyes. I hadn't let Aidan into the room because I'd been too depressed to talk, but he'd been trying to find a way to make me feel better?

"I agree with Del," Nix said. "That locket has to be a clue. You were wearing it when you woke in the field fifteen years ago, and you've guarded it ever since. If it played a role in your dream, it's important."

"So what do you suggest I do about it?" I asked.

"Hunt down some information. Learn what you can about your past. Go from there."

My past. A flare of purpose ignited in my chest. I'd had a power that was stolen, or lost. Maybe I could get it back. Or at least learn about what had happened to me. It was better than moping around here all the time.

"And maybe you can find a way to get your powers back," Nix said.

"It's not possible," I said.

"You don't know that. Anything is possible."

Getting my powers back. Hope flared in my chest, a bright light that drove out some of the dark.

"I agree with Nix," Del said. "You should try to get your powers back."

"But how?"

"I don't know," Del said. "Start with learning about your past and your stolen root power. Your locket may be a clue, considering how it reacted when the Monster tried to steal your power. Maybe that will lead you somewhere."

It might. And I wanted to learn about my past. Aethelred was the first person I'd ever met who might know something. Now I had a lead, at least.

Maybe getting my powers back was a stretch. But it didn't mean I couldn't try.

"You need to do it," Del said. "The Monster won't stop coming. You heard what the seer said. He's up to something big, even if we don't know what it is yet. And you can't exactly hang around without your powers."

"You're right." I'd do anything to get them back. "Thanks for helping me get my head out of my butt."

Del shrugged. "It's cool. If I'd gone through what you have, I'd be acting the same."

"Likewise," Nix said.

"Thanks." I reached out and squeezed both of their hands, then climbed off the bed. "Okay, time for me to get back to the world of the living. I need a shower. I don't think my dip in the Pool of Enchantment counted."

I only cried a little bit in the shower, but by the time I got out, I felt a lot better. My chest still felt empty, but that just left more room for the hope to grow.

I laughed at my bad poetry and went into the bedroom. A fresh change of clothes lay on the bed, along with my two daggers. I tugged on clothes, then reached for Lefty and Righty, grateful I hadn't lost them during my griffin changes. I was going to need them now. I'd lasted a long time without my magic. I could do it again.

I hefted their familiar weight and tossed the blades into the air, watching the black glass glimmer in the light before catching them. After strapping the daggers to my thighs, I headed out in search of Aidan.

I found him in the kitchen, unloading bags of ice cream into the freezer.

"What are those for?" I asked.

He spun, a grin on his face. His gray eyes roved over me, relief clear in their depths.

"They were for you, but since you're up and about, maybe you don't need them."

"Hey now." I approached and hopped up on the island counter across from him. "Can't take them back."

"All right." He stepped close, and my heart raced.

The memory of his kisses the other night made my skin heat. I grabbed his shirt and tugged him closer.

"But you'll have to earn them," he said.

"How?"

"Go talk to Aethelred about your locket."

I'd been hoping he'd say I had to earn them with kisses or something fun like that, but the fact that he wanted me to hunt down my past made my heart flutter.

"You're a good guy, Aidan Merrick. Are you sure you don't have an ulterior motive?"

"'Course I do." He grinned, so handsome I wanted to eat him up. "You being happy seems to make me happy."

"But we haven't even known each other that long."

He rubbed his jaw. "Yeah, that's the weird thing." He shrugged. "It just doesn't seem to matter. You're the strongest, bravest person I've ever met, and apparently I have a thing for that."

I grinned, my empty chest not hurting quite so much. "Fine. I'll go to Aethelred. I want to learn about my past. And try to get my powers back."

A shadow crossed Aidan's face, as if he doubted my odds at getting my powers back. Then he grinned. "Good. If there's a way to do it, you'll find it."

"Thanks."

"There is one thing, though," Aidan said. "The Order of the Magica wants to meet the people who helped me with the portal. To thank you. They would make it part of the ceremony for the Nullifier."

I jerked back. "Hell no."

"You could get credit for saving Magic's Bend."

That was appealing. Getting on the Order's good side could only help me in the future, on the off-chance they figured out what I was. "I suppose I could do it before I get my power back. Now that I'm just a void of nullification, they won't be able to sense my FireSoul."

"I like how you think."

"Yeah?"

"Yeah. You'll get your power back, but until then, you'll take advantage of what you've got going for you."

"I'd better get my power back." I clenched my fists in his shirt. "It's part of me. I feel like hell now that it's gone."

And I couldn't be an immortal. It was like the worst life-sentence ever. Eternal loneliness once my *deirfiúr* and Aidan died. Just the thought made me sweat.

"Good. You're going to need it." Aidan's face turned grave. "Dr. Garriso called. He said that Victor Orriordor succeeded in taking the Chalice of Youth."

My breath escaped me. "No. Nothing can be stolen from the museum."

"I know. That's how it's supposed to work. But something must have happened while part of the museum disappeared at the waypoint. The chalice was stolen."

Shit. "So we failed."

"You saved the museum. Hundreds of lives. That's not failure."

I nodded, but the idea of the Monster getting what he was after made my head spin. Why did he need the immortality gifted by the chalice if he was already immortal? What horrible thing did he have planned?

"We'll handle this, Cass. Whatever the Monster's end goal, we'll stop it. No matter what we have to do."

I hoped he was right. I had to handle it. And get my powers back. Because living like this wasn't an option.

THANK YOU FOR READING!

I hope you liked *Stolen Magic*. Reviews are *so* helpful to authors. I really appreciate all reviews, both positive and negative.

The sequel to *Stolen Magic* will be available early August. Join my newsletter to find out more. I love hearing from readers. You can contact me at Linsey@LinseyHall.com.

If you'd like to know more about the inspiration for the Dragon's Gift series, please read on for the Author's Note.

AUTHOR'S NOTE

I hope you enjoyed reading *Stolen Magic* as much as I enjoyed writing it. Writing Cass's adventures are a labor of love for me because in addition to being a writer, I am also an archaeologist. The Dragon's Gift series allows me to combine my two loves—writing and history—which has been amazing.

As with my other stories, *Stolen Magic* features historical sites. The most important historical site in *Stolen Magic* is the Museum of Magical History, which is a based off the Natural History Museum in London. It's an amazing museum, but the building itself is also historic. It was completed in 1881 and features incredible architecture that made it a perfect setting for Cass's third adventure. Not only is it full of old stuff, the building is technically also old stuff as well.

For the purposes of the story, I cleared out all the dinosaur skeletons and replaced the collections with magical archaeological artifacts. The cover image is meant to be one of the windows of the museum's main hall, though I'll confess that we actually used an image of

Holyrood Abbey in Edinburgh because it worked better from an artistic standpoint.

But one of the most important things about the Dragon's Gift series is Cass's relationship with the artifacts and the sense of responsibility she feels to protect them. I spoke about this in the Author's Note for *Ancient Magic* and *Mirror Mage*, so this might be repetitive for some folks (feel free to quit now if so), but I want to include it in each of my Author's Notes because it's so important to me.

I knew I had a careful line to tread when writing these books—combining the ethics of archaeology with the fantasy aspect of treasure hunting isn't always easy.

There is a big difference between these two activities. As much as I value artifacts, they are not treasure. Not even the gold artifacts. They are pieces of our history that contain valuable information, and as such, they belong to all of us. Every artifact that is excavated should be properly conserved and stored in a museum so that everyone can have access to our history. No one single person can own history, and I believe very strongly that individuals should not own artifacts. Treasure hunting is the pursuit of artifacts for personal gain.

So why did I make Cass Cleraux a treasure hunter? I'd have loved to call her an archaeologist, but nothing about Cass's work is like archaeology. Archaeology is a very laborious, painstaking process—and it certainly doesn't involve selling artifacts. That wouldn't work for the fast paced, adventurous series that I had planned for Dragon's Gift. Not to mention the fact that dragons are famous for coveting treasure. Considering where Cass got her skills from, it just made sense to call her a treasure hunter (though I really like to think of her as a magic hunter). Even though I write urban fantasy, I strive for accuracy. Cass doesn't engage in archaeological practices—therefore, I cannot call her an archaeologist. I also have a duty as an archaeologist to properly represent my field and our goals—namely, to protect and share history. Treasure hunting doesn't do this. One of the biggest battles that archaeology faces today is protecting cultural heritage from thieves.

I debated long and hard about not only what to call Cass, but also about how she would do her job. I wanted it to involve all the cool things we think about when we think about archaeology—namely, the Indiana Jones stuff, whether it's real or not. Because that stuff is fun, and my main goal is to write a fun book. But I didn't know quite how to do that while still staying within the bounds of my own ethics. I can cut myself and other writers some slack because this is fiction, but I couldn't go too far into smash and grab treasure hunting.

I consulted some of my archaeology colleagues to get their take, which was immensely helpful. Wayne Lusardi, the State Maritime Archaeologist for Michigan, and Douglas Inglis and Veronica Morris, both archaeologists for Interactive Heritage, were immensely helpful with ideas. My biggest problem was figuring out how to have Cass steal artifacts from tombs and then sell them and still sleep at night. Everything I've just said is pretty counter to this, right?

That's where the magic comes in. Cass isn't after the artifacts themselves (she puts them back where she found them, if you recall)—she's after the magic that the artifacts contain. She's more of a magic hunter than a treasure hunter. That solved a big part of my problem. At least she was putting the artifacts back. Though that's not proper archaeology (especially the damage she sometimes causes, which she always goes back to fix), I could let it pass. At least it's clear that she believes she shouldn't keep the artifact or harm the site. But the SuperNerd in me said, "Well, that magic is part of the artifact's context. It's important to the artifact and shouldn't be removed and sold."

Now *that* was a problem. I couldn't escape my SuperNerd self, so I was in a real conundrum. Fortunately, that's where the immensely intelligent Wayne Lusardi came in. He suggested that the magic could have an expiration date. If the magic wasn't used before it decayed, it could cause huge problems. Think explosions and tornado spells run amok. It could ruin the entire site, not to mention possibly cause injury and death. That would be very bad.

So now you see why Cass Clereaux didn't just steal artifacts to sell them. Not only is selling the magic cooler, it's also better from an ethical standpoint, especially if the magic was going to cause problems in the long run. These aren't perfect solutions—the perfect solution would be sending in a team of archaeologists to carefully record the site and remove the dangerous magic—but that wouldn't be a very fun book. Hopefully this was a good compromise that you enjoyed (and that my old professors don't hang their heads over).

ABOUT LINSEY

Before becoming a writer, Linsey was an archaeologist who studied shipwrecks in all kinds of water, from the tropics to muddy rivers (and she has a distinct preference for one over the other). After a decade of tromping around in search of old bits of stuff, she settled down to started penning her own adventure novels and is freaking delighted that people seem to like them. Since life is better with a little (or a lot of) magic, she writes urban fantasy and paranormal romance.

Copyright 2016 by Linsey Hall
Published by Bonnie Doon Press LLC

Linsey@LinseyHall.com
www.LinseyHall.com
https://twitter.com/HiLinseyHall
https://www.facebook.com/LinseyHallAuthor

BONNIE
DOON
PRESS

ISBN 978-1-942085-26-3

61780000R00156

Made in the USA
Middletown, DE
14 January 2018